A BLACK MAGICIAN CALLED
SNYDER
A Legend In The Segregated South

WILLIE JAMES WEBB

A BLACK MAGICIAN CALLED SNYDER

A Legend In The Segregated South

WILLIE JAMES WEBB

HOLY BIBLE
WILLIE JAMES WEBB

CONTENTS

PREFACE

Imagine being a negro child growing up in Macon County, Alabama, in the 1930s where Booker T. Washington built Tuskegee Institute University, hired George Washington Carver, and established John Andrews Community Hospital operated predominantly by Black American physicians during this time period. Furthermore, imagine that you as a child attended a segregated school of committed teachers who were dedicated with a zeal and passion for knowledge and learning was an exciting experience. That was the atmosphere in the Rosenwald schools during this time period in Macon County beginning in early 1900s.

Imagine that you are immersed in a rich culture of Black pride, Black beauty, Black hope, and Black excellence. Immersed in such a rich culture, it is no wonder that a Black heroic magician, such as Snyder, would emerge. This was a culture that instilled hope and faith in God that made all things seem possible. So when Snyder the magician visited your school, this was consistent with your hope, your faith that all things are possible for those who believe in God. It was an empowering culture with survival values in a hostile world.

Considering the large number of Black American heroes that emerged in the early nineteenth century was consistent with this atmosphere of "Black Magic." Consider Frederick Douglas, Booker T. Washington, George Washington Carver, Joe Louis, Paul Roberson, Jesse Owens, Paul Lawrence Dunbar, and the Tuskegee Airmen. Consider Harriet Tubman, Mary McLeod Bethune, Lena Horn, Mahalia Jackson, and a host of others who created this rich culture and atmosphere of magic, hope, and high expectations and accomplishments.

Considering this rich, creative, and hopeful magic-like atmosphere and culture, the Black heroic Magician Snyder emerged as an embodiment of the fertile pristine Black American culture existing at Tuskegee, Norasulga, Macon County, and other areas in Alabama at this time in history. Yes, Snyder was a unique individual Black man. However, as we read the Legends of Snyder: A Heroic Black Magician, let us be reminded that there was something in the quality and spirit of this East Alabama culture that produced many other unique individuals that are not necessarily recorded in the history books.

W. J. Demus Webb
Theological Ethicist

INTRODUCTION

When I consider the early superheroes of my childhood, many men come to my mind. I recall walking long distances with older siblings and friends to listen to the prize fights of Joe Louis by the radio. It was always a spectacular event to hear of the competitive spirit and punching power of the man called "The Brown Bomber." Joe Louis was one of my early superheroes.

I was fascinated with what George Washington Carver, the Black scientist at Tuskegee, could do with the peanut. The extraordinary struggle of Booker T. Washington to get an education has inspired me from boyhood to adulthood. He overcame his slave background and insurmountable odds and founded Tuskegee Institute College in Tuskegee, Alabama, in 1881.

My respect and admiration for these men loom large because of the time, place, and circumstances surrounding their contributions. My being a native of the state of Alabama increased my affinity with them because of their association with Alabama.

Abraham Lincoln, the man who is credited with freeing the Negro slaves in America, was also a superhero of my youth. There were others, including the legendary John Henry, the steel-driving man.

My curiosity concerning these men was subsequently satisfied by the history books and the continuous flow and availability of information concerning them. But there was another superhero of my youth that was left out of the history books and the printed press. This man could very well be one of the most unusual and unique men of Black American history.

After finishing college, earning two master's degrees, marrying and raising a daughter to adulthood, still, sufficient curiosity remained about this unrecorded unique man to launch an investigation after forty years to satisfy my curiosity. The years had not erased from my memory, nor the memory of others, the mysterious works of a Black man called Snyder.

As a child, I had heard from numerous people about the many fantastic and incredible things that this man did. All agreed that they had not seen or heard of anyone else who could do the things that he did.

Those who saw him expressed astonishment at his ability to cause extraordinary happenings that defied logic and reason. He fascinated the imagination of young people. He invoked awe, amazement, mystery, and wonderment among those who saw him. Brave men expressed respect, curiosity, apprehension, reverence, and sometimes fear in the presence of this strange man. Many people stated that they preferred keeping a safe distance from Snyder. He excited, astonished, hypnotized, and mystified masses of people.

During my investigation of this man, I was amazed over and over again how well people remembered him. Even after forty-five years some people talk about the things he did with such enthusiasm and excitement that one is led to believe that this man must have been very extraordinary.

Snyder left lasting impressions on people. Memories of him and what he did are among the most vivid impressions of the people who saw him. The general impression of the people who saw him is characterized by fascination, good feelings, thoughts, and a sense of wonder. It's characterized by a positive influence and Black racial pride.

The effects that he had on the people who saw him were so profound that when his name is called many of them light up with excitement. Many start talking spontaneously about the incredible performances they witnessed. All of the people that I spoke with stated that they saw him do impossible things before their very eyes. They reported that these things were so incredible that they could not believe their eyes or ears. And yet the things he did were so visible, so real, and so open and personally witnessed by so many people that to deny what he did would be to deny the reality of one's own sensory perceptions.

The evidence of the existence and actions of this man is real and overwhelmingly convincing. The evidence con- sists not of just specific places, names, and dates and persons, although these exist in abundance. The more significant evidence is found in the common response of a wide variety of people known for their honesty and credibility.

These personal responses came from a wide variety of people. Many of them do not know each other. It is amazing that all of them give invariably the same consistent reports after thirty, forty, and fifty years. They talk about Snyder with a contagious excitement, bold honesty, and conviction that what they saw was real.

On number of occasions, I have talked with two or more persons simultaneously about Snyder without them having knowledge that the other knew him. Enthusiastic conversation with an animated eagerness to relate what each saw Snyder do ensues. One person can hardly wait for the other to finish before he starts telling of things he witnessed.

The things that they relate are interesting and incredible. Their getting caught up with such enthusiasm becomes an extraordinary interest within itself. They express an extraordinary amazement and fascination about things they saw forty years ago as if they happened yesterday.

The memories of this unusual man and the things he did seem to be dormant in the minds of persons who saw him but are revived and renewed in a matter of seconds. Their faces light up with a happy glow of pleasant excitement. Invariably, they start sharing their incredible story about a Black man called Snyder. The story is always characterized by excitement, amazement, and astonishment.

The fact that such deep emotions are aroused after forty years seems to suggest that at some point in time an event of extreme magnitude registered in their minds and hearts and left them with an indelible impression. In spite of the passage of time and the multiplicity of outstanding characters and historical events, the memories of this man persist. The impact of Snyder's performances and his personality are still felt by those who witnessed the unusual things he did.

Another striking uniqueness of Snyder is the large number and variety of incredible and unnatural things that he did. He performed the unnatural and unbelievable in almost every place and every situation he found himself. He was an entertainer, but much more. He took his stage with him everywhere he went. He performed in homes, schools, social gatherings, and up and down the streets in the small towns where he traveled. He became the center of attraction every- where he went. He mystified and mesmerized his audience whether large or small. The people were convinced that this man could do anything.

The existence and actions of this unique individual is further substantiated by his conflicts with the legal authorities. There are reports that he was arrested in the towns of Notasulga, Auburn, and Tuskegee, Alabama. He could not be kept in jail. He released himself from jail by obtaining the keys in a mysterious way and then handed them back to the surprised sheriffs. More incredible than his getting the keys from the sheriff was his getting the sheriff's pistol out of its holster at more than twenty feet away and repelling the bullets fired at him by the police. There are reports that police shot at him and the bullets came back in their direction.

The public appearances of this individual started around 1929 and continued into the early 1940s. He frequently went around the small townships in east Alabama. He visited many of the rural Black schools. He performed a lot on the streets where crowds gathered. This was often on Saturdays when Blacks came to town to shop, associate, and have some outlets from their labors, mostly sharecrop farming. During these times it was common for many Black Americans to stand around, sit around, and socialize on certain street corners.

Towns and cities have historically had a special attraction for Black Americans. It has been a meeting place. It has offered an opportunity to congregate, spectate, observe commerce, and dream of owning some of the wealth and affluence that can be seen in the towns and cities. These were the kind of crowds that made up the audience for the man that possessed magical powers. Remember, there were no televisions, computers, or cell phones. There were only a few radios and a few landline telephones owned by White people mostly.

It seems that this magician or miracle worker appeared at a most unlikely time in American history. This fact further accentuates his extraordinary personality. It was an unlikely time because in 1929 was the beginning of the Great Depression. It was an unlikely time, because racial segregation and discrimination were rampant in the nation, and especially in the South and particularly in Alabama, where this man traveled and performed.

During this time period in American history, it was common for Black people to be insulted, slapped, kicked, beat-lynched, and to suffer endless degrading indignities. Blacks, and especially Black men, were not afforded any respect for the human dignity, of a man among men, or a human being in most cases.

Black men were referred to by White as "boy," "nigger," "John," and other negatively connoted titles. Black people were always vulnerable to having their human rights violated by White persons and rarely have recourses for legal protection during this period in history.

However, there was a mysterious Black man who traveled around the towns, schools, and churches of Alabama among the Black community, who had a power that made him invulnerable to injuries attempted by Whites.

Many of the White people who saw Snyder perform expressed the same respect, reverence, and fear expressed by Blacks. Many Whites watched and enjoyed the performances along with Blacks.

Those Whites, usually the local sheriff or police, who tried to run him out of town would usually end up frustrated, humiliated, and intimidated after learning their powerlessness to exercise any control over this Black man.

During this gloomy period of economic depression and Black human degradation, Snyder provided a diversion from the unpleasant side of life and gave some hope against years of oppression. He was a Black man with invincible powers. He used his magical powers primarily for entertainment.

It must be noted that during the 1930s in rural Alabama there were no sophisticated machinery or electronic devices or any other scientific instruments to assist Snyder in his extraordinary performances. He had no elaborate stage or setups. Most of his performances were outside, on the streets in broad open daylight, surrounded by people. The instruments that he used in his performances were available for examination. His observers saw no evidence of tricks. They were convinced that what they saw was real.

Harry Houdini (1874-1926) was known as one of the greatest magicians of his time. He was famous for perform- ing dangerous feats. He was able to free himself from ropes, handcuffs, chains, boxes that had been nailed shut, and various other kinds of restraints. Although Houdini and Snyder of Alabama were contemporaries, there are no books and no printed references about the latter. And yet the feats that Snyder did were just as unusual, and much more varied, and more mysterious than those done by Houdini. This is not a detraction from the great feats of Houdini. It is a footnote that there was another magician who performed unnatural feats that was not picked up by the recorders of history.

This Alabama mysterious individual was a six-foot-tall Black man with dark skin. He weighed about 180 lbs. He was between forty and fifty years of age when he performed in the 1930s and 1940s. He had no particular physical characteristics that distinguished him from other Black men during that time. He dressed well and drove an automobile around the rural Black schools and country towns. On some occasions, a woman companion traveled with him.

His uniqueness is not found in his physical appearance but rather in the things he did and the personality he projected. Most of the people who knew him state that he was just an ordinary-looking man.

This ordinary-looking Black man established in the minds of those who saw him a positive identity and good reputation. No negative reports could be found about him. Most of the people who saw him perform report that they did not pay anything to see him. Many, if not most, of his performances were street open-air performances where crowds gathered spontaneously.

He was interested in entertainment. He was interested in making people happy through mysterious acts of fascination. He also enjoyed his own performances. As he performed, he was often making fun with the children with humorous statements and magic. Many people acknowledge what he could have become wealthy by his performances or by swindling if he had chosen to do so.

There is evidence to suggest that Snyder practiced high ethical and moral standards. He attended many of the Black churches. He did not allow profanity at his shows or during performances. He gave the impression of being a good- hearted person. He was not associated with voodoo or witchcraft. He was not known to cheat or take the advantage of anyone. He used his powers to entertain, teach, chastise, and, on some occasions, to defend his person and dignity.

The people in my community did not know his real name. They called him Snyder. When he gave a performance, he became the talk of the town. I would often hear my older brothers and sister and other acquaintances talk about the impossible things that Snyder did. My imagination and curiosity were magnified beyond the most exaggerated fantasy. To me, Snyder was a mystery, a Black superhero, a true magician, a man endowed with strange powers, and a factual leg- end found in the oral history of residents of East Alabama.

The things he did were too impossible to be real. And yet they seemed too real to be lies. They were too concrete to be illusions. They were too open and external to be imaginary or hypnotic. There were too many eyewitnesses expand- ing more than a fifteen-year period at specific places, times, and under such a variety of circumstances to conclude that Snyder was fictitious or mythological. He is more recent than Houdini. He is more recent than Booker T. Washington.

Snyder's existence and actions are rooted in real situations, specific places, and times. He is a part of that social fabric that was woven into the subculture of my childhood world. He came along at a time when many Black youths were in need of a Black hero outside of the depressing and limiting conventional imaginary realms. He represented a Black magic that was unmatchable. He represented a Black power that was invincible.

I do not know the mind or the soul of Snyder, but I do know that the things he did had significant social and psychic impact on those who witnessed them. This book is based on numerous testimonies of credible witnesses, whom I know personally to be truthful and reliable. Many of the people who witnessed the incredible performances are alive to this day. (This research was done in the 1980s and 1990s.)

Some of the names and places mentioned in this book have been changed. Some constructive details and general- ities have been added. However, as the investigator, social researcher, and personal acquaintance of hundreds of the witnesses, I am convinced that the man known as Snyder is a real, unique, and extraordinary personality. I am further convinced that he did things that constituted supernatural happenings that are still shrouded in mystery.

As a boy I saw Snyder as a Black superhero with strange supernatural powers. My boyhood perception has been con- firmed through my own research and investigation. I found nothing illegal, immoral, or unethical in the public life of Snyder. This strange Black man with his extraordinary mag- ical expertise brought great entertainment, hope, and racial pride to many, and especially Black people and Black children in the Rosenwald schools in Macon County, Lee County, and surrounding counties in East Alabama.

This social research and investigation took place between the 1980s and 1990s. During this ten-year period, I would drive from Atlanta, Georgia, to the townships in Alabama, where I was born and reared through high school at Tuskegee Institute; the townships of Tuskegee, Notasulga, Montgomery, Loachapoka, Auburn, and Opelika, Alabama.

Most of the people that I talked with and interviewed were persons that I know personally. They were my elders as I was growing up as a child, and they were aware and in tune with what was going on in the community when I was a child. Their honesty and credibility were unquestionable.

I am convinced, after an extensive investigation into the life and performances of Snyder, that he exhibited positive and ethical behavior. There was no indication from anyone that I spoke with that expressed anything negative about the man known as Snyder. There was no indication that he did any harm to anyone. He enjoyed making people happy with his magic. Even when he used his magic to defend himself from the racial aggression of the White persons and White authorities, he did not hurt them physically. He confounded them by using his magic in the process.

The stories of Snyder related in this book are based on the information shared with me during my investigation into the life and legends of a man called Snyder. There was a lot of fascinating storytelling during my youth that intrigued and excited the imagination. We had no television to watch in the 1930s and 1940s in my community in Macon Country, Alabama. Our entertainment was live. Snyder was a live entertainment event that took place over several decades. It was a healthy diversion from the racial inequalities and indignities of the rigid realities of racial segregation and deprivations in East Alabama.

There were ethical considerations that I had to reconcile before the publication of this book could be submitted. The information about Snyder had to conform to truth and honesty. Also, the book must be positive with redeeming educational and civilized social values. In addition to entertainment, the book must have positive messages and themes that are beneficial to humanity. It must teach relevant lessons that enhance life and elevate humanity. It must be a bona fide part of the Black American experience and culture of America.

My rigorous ethical and moral evaluations and assessments of the legends of Snyder were overwhelmingly positive. I could not find a single person who spoke negatively about Snyder. They were all positive and favorable. All the Black persons that I talked with about Snyder were positive and expressed good and pleasant experiences regarding Snyder. As a youth, Snyder became one of my heroes through hearing older siblings and others talk about his amazing feats as a magician and entertainer. My later investigations about the legends of Snyder confirmed my positive childhood impressions of a Black man and Black magician called Snyder.

It is not possible or historically responsible to talk about the happenings in Macon County, Alabama, the municipal home and country seat of Tuskegee, without alluding to the works and the international influence of Booker T. Washington and George Washington Carver. In addition to the founding of Tuskegee Institute in 1881, Booker T. Washington, in conjunction with Julius Rosenwald, established 4,500 schools throughout fifteen southern states in America. Shiloh Elementary in Notasulga was one of those schools founded in 1922. This was one of the Rosenwald schools for Black children where Snyder performed for the students on a number of occasions.

The Shiloh Rosenwald School, Shiloh Baptist Church, and the Shiloh Cemetery are national historic sites. Shiloh School was born out of Shiloh Baptist Church located approximately four miles from the Tuskegee Airmen's Moton Field.

Moton Field was the air base where the Tuskegee airman trained to fly military airplanes. During the 1940s it was fascinating as a child to watch the Black American pilots to fly the Tuskegee air force planes. As a child growing up within six miles of Moton Field, I observed the Black American pilots perform many interesting aviation maneuvers in the sky. I have seen them cut the motors off and allow the plane to begin falling from the sky, and then suddenly restart the engine and stop the falling of the plane from a descending nosedive to an upward ascent back into the sky. I have seen the Tuskegee airmen do a complete revolution in the sky, a "loop the loop." This was rich entertainment for the children in the Rosenwald schools.

The name "Rosenwald School" was not known publicly. These segregated schools took their names from the churches where they were located. It has been within the past thirty years (from 1970s) that knowledge of the 4,500 Rosenwald schools have come to the forefront. These Rosenwald schools started as significant relationship between the Black church and the Black schools. There are many lessons and blessings that have resulted from this educational and religious relationship. It also provided opportunities for Black American school children to be exposed to unusual and gifted individuals, such as Snyder.

I am grateful for those men and women who shared their knowledge and personal observation of the most unusual magician, entertainer, and Black American man of the entertainment industry. I am also grateful for the rich, stimulating, and fascinating individual known as Snyder.

It is hoped that the Legends of Snyder: A Black Heroic Magician will provide, vicariously, some of the fascination and entertaining excitement of those who witnessed the magical performances of Snyder in the segregated south of East Alabama, in the decades of the 1920s, 1930s, and 1940s. It is also hoped that some appreciation will be given to the extraordinary and varied artistic abilities of the Black Americans in so many enriched areas of their lives and the Southern American culture.

This book is about an extraordinary Black American man who was gifted with the ability to perform magical performances. However, I was blessed to be reared in a culture that produced many renowned and outstanding individuals. Snyder performed in the areas of Alabama that were influenced by Booker T. Washington, George Washington Carver, and others. God has provided many great men and women for humanity. Many of their names and contributions are lost in history.

CHAPTER 1

Money Came Down Like Rain

A group of Black men of various ages were standing around talking and socializing as they usually did on Saturdays in the small town of Notasulga. In this small town, there were certain corners and streets where various groups would congregate, especially on Saturdays, when most of the shopping was done. A Black man drove up in an old Buick automobile. He got out of the car and joined the group of men.

After a brief conversation, this man who got out of the car asked one of the men in the group to lend him five dollars. The man answered and said he did not have it.

Snyder told the man exactly how much money he had in his pocket. The man was astonished beyond belief. This caught the attention of others in the group. They became skeptical and curious.

Different ones in the group started asking Snyder to guess how much money each had in his pocket. Snyder would tell them the exact amount each time.

Another unbelieving man came up and told Snyder, "I bet you can't tell me how much money I got."

Snyder told the man that he had eleven dollars.

The man started laughing and told Snyder that he missed it.

The man said he only had six dollars.

Snyder told him that he had a five-dollar bill in his right shoe.

The man continued to laugh and told the group that he knew well that he did not have a five-dollar bill in his right shoe. The man pulled his right shoe off and a five-dollar bill was in the shoe. The man was speechless. The group was amazed. At that point, Snyder had become a street entertainer. Other persons passing by began stopping to observe the interesting spectacle that was taking place. Some Whites, women, and children started gathering around.

Snyder called a little boy who was about ten years old to come shake his hand. This little boy came to him. Snyder told him that he was going to give him some money. He placed fifty cents in the boy's hand and told him to hold it real tight and not lose it. The boy continued to hold the fifty cents while Snyder continued to carry on the fun with the crowd.

Snyder turned to the boy a few seconds later and asked him if he had lost the fifty cents.

The little boy answered, "No, sir."

Snyder said, "Okay, let me see it."

The boy opened his hand, and it was empty. Puzzlement and amusement came to the face of the little boy. The boy and the crowd were more puzzled when Snyder asked another boy on the opposite side of the crowd to reach into his back pocket and give the ten-year-old his fifty cents back. To his astonishment, the second boy found the fifty cents in his back pocket.

Snyder asked several men to "let me see your pocketbook." The men found to their unpleasant surprise that their pocketbooks were no longer in their usual pockets. Some of the wallets were found in the pockets of others.

This unusual power of Snyder caused some of the bystanders to keep a safe distance from Snyder as demonstrated by some who would not get close enough to participate in the unusual activities.

Snyder asked a lady in the group "Please, madam, give me a one-dollar bill for some change."

The lady handed him the dollar bill and it changed to a five-dollar bill before it left her hand.

He asked her, "Miss, do you have a one-dollar bill?"

She could not believe her eyes. She had pulled out a one-dollar bill, but it was a five-dollar bill she put back in her pocketbook.

Within thirty minutes of Snyder's arrival in this small Alabama town, over seventy-five people had gathered around him. This had become the largest attraction in this town. The interest, curiosity, and apprehension of many persons had been stirred. There were whispers in the crowd. "Who is this man?" "Where did this Negro come from?" "How in the world does he do those things?"

The Blacks were thoroughly enjoying this entertainment by Snyder. Some of the Whites were also. However, the White leadership, which involved several store owners, owners of the larger farms, and other well-known Whites, felt that this man should be watched. So they asked the one police in the town to keep an eye on the situation. As he was instructed, the White police came where the crowd was to keep an eye on Snyder and to also disperse the crowd without any trouble.

Snyder was still having fun with the people, causing money to appear and disappear. He borrowed a man's hat. He gave a young boy three one-dollar bills and told him to put them down on the street. He asked another youth to place the hat over the money. He asked a third youth to take the hat from over the money. When the third youth picked the hat up, the money was not there. Snyder asked the youth to search for the hat. He did so, and the money was not there. Snyder got one of the dollar bills out of the first boy's ears, another from the second boy's nose, and the third dollar bill from the third boy's mouth. The crowd laughed with amusement.

Snyder got a lady's ring and a man's watch and placed them under the hat. He asked one of the boys to raise the hat. The watch and ring had disappeared. He instructed him to put the hat back on the ground. The boy did so. He asked him to raise the hat again. The boy raised the hat the second time, and the ring and watch were under the hat. He instructed the boy to place the hat over the ring and watch again. He then asked him to lift the hat. The watch was there, but the ring was not. Snyder looked puzzled. He looked at the woman, who owned the ring, in an effort, to give her some assurance.

Snyder returned the man's watch and got the hat, looked in it, and shook it and the ring could not be found. He told the lady that he had looked everywhere and could not find it and suggested that she look in her pocketbook.

The lady looked in her pocketbook and to her astonishment the ring was there. The crowd saw it, but they could not believe it.

Snyder saw a White man with a pocket watch in his vest pocket. He asked the man what time it was. When the man pulled his watch out, Snyder asked the man to let him see the watch. The man handed it to him. Snyder threw the watch to the concrete sidewalk, and the gold watch broke and scattered in every direction. The White man became visibly angry and asked Snyder, "Boy, do you know how much that watch costs?" The crowd began to get a little tense because a Black man had done something to offend a White man. The White police nervously made his way closer to the center of the attraction.

Snyder told the White man that he did not want to buy his watch but that he would see if he could fix it. Snyder knelt and picked the pieces up and put them in a handkerchief, wrapped the pieces in the handkerchief, and the watch was as good as new. It was ticking and had not lost any time.

The crowd again was amazed, and they expressed a sigh of relief that the White man's watch was returned undamaged. The crowd had increased to over a hundred people, White and Black. That was a large crowd in a town with a population of five hundred people.

The police felt that it was about time for him to do something because a large crowd is a threat to law and order. Also, Whites and Blacks are standing in a semi-mixed audience. Snyder has so dazzled their imagination that the racial tension had been minimized. The Whites and Blacks have suspended temporarily their suspicions and fears. They are being entertained by an unusual and even strange Black man. A semi-mixed audience like this does not reflect well on their system of segregation and discrimination against Blacks, Not only that, but the center of attraction is a Black man. This Black man is not helping the wide-held perception that Blacks are inferior. The police felt the town rulers could not tolerate a situation like this. And it was his responsibility to do something about it.

However, this Black man had demonstrated an unusual ability and even a strange power. For these reasons, the police were under restraints to proceed cautiously. The police also had some of the same apprehensions and underlying fears about Snyder as the other people who were watching him. This added to the difficulty and awkwardness of his approaching Snyder. However, the pressure of the law, authority, and local traditions compelled the police to approach Snyder. His approach was much milder than he preferred. Ordinarily, the police officer would have been very direct, insulting, and threatening to a Black man. Ordinarily, he would have addressed him as "Nigger" and commanded him to get out of town. However, the policeman perceived something unusual about this man. Nevertheless, he must do what was expected of him as a White police officer in a Southern rural town.

The police officer walked up in front of Snyder and told him that he would have to charge him ten dollars for showing up on the street. Snyder told the police that he was just having some fun with the people free of charge and did not feel that he should give him ten dollars.

It was highly provocative and intolerable for a Black man to disagree with a White man in this small town. Black men were often beaten and even killed for openly disagreeing with a White man, especially with a policeman.

Snyder had just openly disagreed with the police. The policeman was provoked. He told Snyder that he must pay the ten dollars or be arrested.

Snyder smiled and told the police officer, "Mr. Police, you can't arrest me." Snyder reached into his pocket and handed a ten-dollar bill to the policeman. The police accepted the ten dollars and put it in his pocket. The police walked off not entirely happy, with the confrontation, but felt that he had gotten a concession by getting the ten dollars he requested.

Before the policeman could walk twenty feet away, Snyder told him to check his pockets to see whether he still had the ten dollars. The police pulled out of his pockets two cigarette leaves in place of the ten-dollar bill. The crowd laughed.

The police felt humiliated, embarrassed, and insulted by this Black man. Snyder's sense of humor and magical powers made it very difficult for the police officer to counter-act because the police did not know how to respond to disagreeable Black men except with threats, intimidation, and violence. Threats and intimidation had not worked against Snyder. The policeman was not sure that violence would work either. He was wearing a .38 revolver, but somehow, he did not feel as powerful and in control of this situation as he wanted to be. The police felt that he must now use his .38 revolver if that becomes necessary to get in control of the situation.

The policemen threw the two cigarette leaves to the ground. With a reddened face, he put his hands on his holster and walked toward Snyder. The people started backing up to make room.

There were several other White men who were known to kick and beat Blacks into their so-called places. However, these White men expressed no eagerness to get involved at this point. They seemed willing to let the policeman handle this unpredictable Black man.

The Whites and Blacks were watching this spectacle, which had developed into a high drama.

They watched with eager anticipation and heightened suspense as the police approached Snyder with his hand on his holstered gun. He stopped about ten feet away from Snyder and told him that he was under arrest.

Snyder told the police, "I know that you don't like me because my skin is black. But I did not come to cause trouble. I am having clean fun with the people."

Snyder told the policeman that he was spoiling the fun and that he wanted the police to help him make the people happy.

Snyder then did an incredible thing that was unthinkable in this small town in 1929.

He told the police to dance.

The police took his hand from his gun and started a fantastic foot dance. He started tap dancing and buck dancing, jumping up and down, swinging his arms and hands with a rhythm characteristic of Black dancing. This dancing by the police created uncontrollable laughter among the Blacks. The reaction of the Whites was surprise, confusion, amazement, and disbelief.

The police continued to dance for several minutes. Snyder asked him if he was tired. He then told him to keep dancing until he told him to stop.

After a few more minutes of dancing, Snyder told him to stop.

The police stopped.

He then told the police to go back where he came from and leave him alone.

The police left and went down the street with the appearance of a man in shock.

The people saw it, but they could not believe that a White man would obey a Black man under any circumstance. And yet this White police in a racist Southern state just a few decades from slavery obeyed the command of a Black man to dance and make a public spectacle of himself. For most people who saw it found it difficult to imagine what had just taken place.

Snyder returned his attention back to the people gathered around him and continued having fun with his magical performances. He asked several little children what they would like to have. Some said candy, some said apples and oranges, and some said money.

Snyder pulled off his hat and held it out showing that it was empty. He also shook the hat to indicate that nothing was in it. He then held the hat up toward the sky and said, "Snyder, send me down some candy."

The sound of things falling in the hat could be heard, and also the hat could be observed moving from the impact of falling objects. Snyder lowered the hat and it was filled with various kinds of candy.

He passed the candy around to the children and also to some of the adults. Some of them ate the candy and some were afraid to eat it.

Snyder held his hat up again and said, "Snyder, send me down some fruits."

The sound and sight of objects falling into the hat could be observed and heard. He lowered the hat, and it was filled with apples, oranges, and grapes. Snyder passed them around to the children and also to the adults.

Some ate them. Some pocketed them. Some examined them with skepticism.

By this time, Snyder had baffled the minds of all those who watched him. They had tried with all their logic and with all their imaginations to figure out how Snyder performed the unbelievable in broad daylight and before their very eyes. After he made the police dance, they were convinced that his powers went beyond trickery and the sleight of the hands.

A White man in rural Alabama in 1929 would not consider lowering himself to participate in any kind of performance with a Black man. The crowd knew that this policeman danced because of the power that Snyder exercised over him. There had been some situations where Whites had intimidated Blacks to the point of forcing them to do embarrassing things, such as dancing, but this was the first time a Black man had made a White man dance in this small town. Snyder continued to do things that defied logic and ordinary comprehension.

Snyder told one of the local Black men by the name of "Mose" to go shake a nearby chinaberry tree that was on the side of the automobile service station. The tree was about dead with very few leaves on it. Mose went over and shook the tree, and silver money started falling from the tree hitting the ground and rolling in every direction. People started running around picking up the money and stuffing their pockets with money also.

Snyder held up his hat and said, "Snyder, I need a little money. Send me down some money."

Money started falling from the sky like rain. The people were fascinated and astonished. They ran around picking up the money and stuffing their pockets and pocketbooks in a sensational frenzy. The money seemed to hit the ground with rattling and jingling sounds but was disappearing like the melting of raindrops.

Suddenly, it stopped. In seconds the money disappeared from the ground. It disappeared from their stuffed pockets. The people witnessed it but could not believe it. They were left speechless wondering what had happened. Wondering what had taken over their behavior. "Where did that money come from? Where did it go?" were their questions.

Snyder waved his hands and said, "Bye-bye, children."

Snyder walked to his car. As he approached the car, the door opened on its own. The motor in the car started on its own. Snyder got in the car and the car drove off.

The people, still speechless, watched Snyder leave. They looked all around. They looked at each other, in an effort, to confirm what each had witnessed but yet so difficult to believe.

They continued to look around and look up in the sky. And one person said as he gave utterance to the thoughts of the others, "Money came down like rain."

CHAPTER 2

A Stove Pipe Overflowing with Fruits and Candies

The word was out that Snyder would be performing at Shiloh School, a Black elementary school, three miles south of Notasulga. This was in the fall of 1935.

This news would invariably generate a lot of excitement among the children as well as the adults. Snyder had a reputation for being a mystery man who could do anything.

The evening finally arrived when Snyder was to appear at the school. It was a three-room, wood-frame, white school building. There was a sliding petition between the two large rooms. They could be converted into one large auditorium. The petition was removed.

Before long a crowd of people had drifted into the school building. They waited eagerly for Snyder to appear.

Finally, the principal of the school came out before the group and conducted a brief devotion consisting of a song and the Lord's Prayer.

She then stated that Snyder would be performing. As she gave the introductory remarks, the anticipation of the group sharpened. Eyes and ears became more alert.

Snyder walked out on the one-foot-high stage. There was no curtain. It was an open stage. He was not a flashy-look- ing man. He looked to be an ordinary middle-aged Black man. He had on an ordinary dark suit, but he was not fancy-dressed.

Snyder told the group that he was there to have good clean fun with them. He told them that he did not permit any cursing or fighting where he performed and no weapons.

One of the students had a red rubber ball in his hand. Snyder asked to see the ball. The boy gave the ball to Snyder.

Snyder threw the ball into the chalkboard. It appeared as if it went into the board, but it did not make any sound. The hole in the board could be observed closing up, until the red ball disappeared into the chalkboard which was in the wall at the back of the stage.

He asked a man in the back row to look into his pocket and get the ball. The man was amazed to find the red rubber ball in his pocket. This was strange and unbelievable to the man and the group.

He asked a man by the name of Ed Ingram, who was seated near the front, to come to a table where Snyder was standing. He asked Ed to let him hold the fifty-cent coin Ed had in his pocket.

Ed gave the coin to Snyder.

Snyder put the coin on the table and told Ed, "I bet this coin knows a lot about you."

Ed looked a little apprehensive and confused. Snyder said, "I believe I'll ask this half-a-dollar coin some questions about you."

Ed laughed. Snyder asked the fifty-cent coin, "Is this an honest man?"

There was no response from the coin.

Snyder asked another question, "Does this man drink liquor?"

The coin on its own jumped up on the table and landed on its head. "Has he had any tonight?"

The coin jumped up and landed on head.

The crowd laughed because they knew that Ed was known to hit the bottle with frequency. At the same time, the group was puzzled by the coin jumping up from the table on its own. The coin was responding to the questions asked by Snyder. "Is this a handsome man?"

The coin did not respond.

The crowd laughed. Ed was mystified. Snyder asked, "Is this a wise man?"

The coin did not respond. "Does this man have another woman?"

The coin jumped up two times and landed on head.

The crowd roared with laughter. Snyder asked Ed, "Shall we ask the coin any more questions?" Ed answered, "No, not about me." Snyder told Ed that the coin belonged to him and asked Ed if he wanted it back. Ed answered, "No, you can have it."

This produced a lot of humor as Ed returned to his seat.

Snyder poured a glass of water from a pitcher and asked if anybody was thirsty. A teenage boy stated that he was thirsty. Snyder asked him to come up and have a drink.

He gave the teenager the glass of water. The teenager put the glass to his mouth and turned it up to drink. To the teenager's surprise, the water would not pour out. The youth kept turning the glass up, but it would not pour out. He turned it upside down. The water would still not pour out.

Another youth in the audience shouted out that he did not believe that there was any water in the glass. Snyder asked him to come up and examine it for himself.

The youth came up and got the glass from the first youth and immediately held the glass up, to look into it, and in the process, the glass of water splashed out in his face. The audience found it hilarious.

Snyder had three pitchers on the table. He poured a glass of water from one pitcher. He poured a glass of milk from the second pitcher. He poured a glass of red Kool-Aid from the third pitcher.

He asked for three volunteers to come up and have them drink of their choice.

It was not easy to get three volunteers. However, after some urging on by various individuals in the audience, three teenagers came up. Each of them drank the contents of the three glasses.

Snyder had them to stand side by side and face the audience. He looked at them and asked them how they felt They stated that they felt full. Snyder patted their stomachs with his hand and stated, "Boys, y'all have been drinking too much. I tell you what I will do. I am going to give you some relief."

Snyder got three cane-looking hollow reeds and stuck them in each boy's stomach. Then he got the glasses that they drank out of and put them on the table in front of the three boys. He placed the glasses at the end of each reed.

Snyder told the audience that he would pump the liquids out of each boy's stomach.

He asked the first boy to stretch his arm straight out from his shoulder. The boy obeyed.

Snyder started raising and lowering the boy's raised arm up and down. After several pumps of the boy's arm, the water started coming out of the reed. He continued until the glass was filled with water.

He proceeded to do the same with the second boy. The crowd was amazed to see the milk being pumped through the reed until the glass was filled.

He continued the same procedure with the third boy. The red Kool-Aid liquid started pouring out of the reed until the glass was filled.

He then pulled the reeds out of the boys' stomachs and asked them if they felt better. They unanimously agreed that they did. These boys saw these things happening, but they could not believe what they were witnessing-neither could the crowd.

Snyder congratulated the three boys for volunteering their services. He told them that they were brave. He commended the audience for their attention and participation.

Snyder walked to the side of the stage and got a stove pipe and brought it to the center of the stage. A stove pipe was very common in the 1930s, especially in the rural areas of Alabama where Snyder performed. This stove pipe was common and ordinary to all of the people in the room. In fact, there were two heaters in the adjoining rooms with exposed stove pipes extending from the top of the wood and coal heaters through the ceiling and through a chimney, on top of the building. The stove pipes and chimney served as a conduit for the smoke and carbon monoxide to escape as the wood and coal burned.

These stove pipes were about two feet long, hollow cylindrical shaped, with openings at both ends. They were made out of a thin sheet of metal, tin, or an alloy. They were usually dark in appearance. The diameter was approximately six inches. The thin, dark, metallic cylindrical stove pipes were considerably light, weighing less than a pound.

As Snyder held the stove pipe, he told the group that he would give all of them something under one condition.

This aroused the curiosity of the group. He told them he would tell them what that condition would be in a few minutes.

He told them that a stove pipe could be used for things other than exhausting smoke and burning fuel.

He held the stove pipe up before the group. He told them that the stove pipe was "clean, empty, and hollow with openings on both sides." To illustrate his point, he looked through the stove pipe at the audience. They saw his face through the opening in the stove pipe. He also put his arm through the pipe.

Snyder laughed and joked with the audience as he talked about the pipe. "I am sure that everyone is convinced that this pipe is empty because there is more hole than pipe. If anyone has any doubts about this stove pipe being empty, you may come up and take a closer look and examine it for yourself."

Most of the people in the audience were skeptical and fearful of getting too close to Snyder. However, a couple of men in the audience went up and examined the stove pipe.

Snyder, again joking with this audience, asked the two men, "Can you fellows find anything more useful to do than examining stove pipes? Do you see anything different up here than you saw back there?"

Snyder stated humorously, "Ladies and gentlemen, a stove pipe is a stove pipe." Then he asked the two men who had examined the stove pipe what it was.

They both answered, "A stove pipe."

Snyder turned to the audience and said, "I told you so." He says, "Okay, I promised to give everyone in this room something. That something is going to come from this empty stove pipe."

The condition for this to happen is this: "I am asking that the ten prettiest girls in the room come to the front and kiss the stove pipe. Shortly you will see the power of kisses from pretty girls."

The girls in the audience started blushing. The manner in which Snyder gave this invitation was appealing. It aroused their interest to respond and to participate. However, there was reluctance, because of their modesty and bashfulness.

To overcome this modesty, Snyder advised that not all the pretty girls come, "just ten."

Finally, ten young women came forth smiling and exhilarating their charm. They marched around and kissed the stove pipe and returned to their seats during which time Snyder was complimenting them on how beautiful they were and how magical their kisses were.

The audience was also amused by the parade of pretty girls. The admiration of the audience generated a sense of pride within the girls and boosted their self-respect, feelings of worth, and significance.

Snyder asked that everyone in the room march around the front and get some candy and fruit from the stove pipe. The people left their seats and began to march around the front.

As each person reached the out-held stove pipe, it started overflowing with apples, oranges, grapefruits, grapes, and various kinds of candy. Each person could get as much as they wanted. Everyone who chose to reach into the overflowing stove pipe received as much fruit and candy as they wanted.

Some of the people ate the fruits and candy. Some of them were afraid to eat them. Some of the people took them home.

The people were amazed and could not figure out how fruits and candy overflowed from an open-end stove pipe.

Many people, to this day, remember this incident and state that they ate some of the fruit and candy.

Snyder had provided the ultimate in entertainment. The people left with good feelings. Their minds were filled with curiosity and wonder. Snyder became the topic of much discussion.

A stove pipe has very few uses. And yet Snyder provided a stove pipe that overflowed with fruits and candy of all descriptions. This entertainment gave the people an exciting diversion from their poverty and their problems. Life can be exciting in a Black-segregated school and segregated society. Entertainment has played a major role in stimulating, motivating, and elevating the minds and thinking of the oppressed Black Americans.

Snyder demonstrated the positive merits of good, clean, and wholesome entertainment. It minimizes and diminishes negative thoughts and bad feelings. Good feelings are incentives for good actions and positive relationships.

CHAPTER 3

A Car Operates without a Driver

It was in the early part of the afternoon in early fall in a small eastern town in Alabama where Phillip was visiting along with some neighbors who were shopping. This was about 1936. It was a Saturday afternoon. The small rural town was crowded. People were doing their fall and winter shopping. It was about the close of the harvest season. The crops had been gathered.

Young Phillip enjoyed going to town. He did a lot of shopping for his mother. Needlessly to say, he did not stay at home a lot. He was usually in the midst of crowds, wherever they were. He had a special attraction to crowds and excitement.

He walked toward the crowd of people that he saw on Main Street in Tuskegee. A large number of Blacks and many Whites had gathered around to see the Black man called Snyder do mysterious things that defied logic and imagination.

Phillip was thrilled again to see Snyder. His young mind was excited and filled with wonder. He was attracted by the incredible performances of

Snyder, but he was somewhat repelled by the mystery. For that reason, Phillip would keep a safe distance, for he feared the unusual and unnatural things that he did not understand.

On this occasion, Snyder was talking to his automobile. It appeared to be a black Buick made in the 1930s.

Snyder told the crowd of people that his car was intelligent and obedient and that it would do whatever he told it to do. In a humorous manner, he asked the question, "Can you say the same of your wives?" There was laughter in the crowd.

He asked the crowd if they wanted to inspect the car. Some of them looked on the inside and underneath and saw nothing unusual about it.

Snyder told the four doors of the car to open. The doors opened one by one by themselves. The people looked in surprise and astonishment.

He told the doors to close one by one. He was on the outside of the car several feet away from the car. The four doors closed, slamming shut, as if by an invisible hand. No one could give an explanation as to how this was done.

He then told the left rear door to open. The left rear door opened. He got in the back seat of the car. The door closed.

From the rear seat, he told the car to drive off. The car rolled off a few feet and stopped when

Snyder told it to do so. He told the car to back up. The car backed up a few feet. He told it to stop. It stopped. He told the people that he was going to ride around town in the back seat.

Snyder sat in the back seat and the car went around the town square as he sat on the back seat. The people were looking, but they could not figure it out, and they could not believe what they were seeing. Snyder got out of the car. He told the crowd of people that not only was his car intelligent and obedient, but it was also reliable and dependable.

To illustrate this reliability, Snyder climbed on top of the car and lay relaxed on his back with his hands underneath his reclined head and told the car, "Let's go for a ride." The car, without anyone inside of it, went around the town square several times and returned to a stop where Snyder got off.

These events took place in broad daylight in a crowded small town. Usually, the case was when crowds of Black people gathered, it became a concern for the police. The police officer would not have advanced notice because

Snyder would just appear without advance notice, and the crowds would gather spontaneously as he performed. Snyder was well into his performance when the crowd got the attention of the policeman. The police and other law enforcement people started looking on from a distance.

Snyder had the car doing various things. The windows would roll up and down. The lights would go on and off at his request. The horn would blow and stop at his request.

These performances were baffling to everyone observing. No one could come up with a logical explanation. This was high entertainment, but also mysterious and scary. Anyone who could make an automobile operate by itself was powerful with strange secrets.

Snyder told the people that his car had other good qualities. He told them that the car was trustworthy. He told the people that if they would practice the good qualities that his car possessed, the world would be a happier and better place to live.

To demonstrate the trustworthiness of his car, he told the crowd of people that he trusted his car to go places by itself and return as he requested.

Snyder stated in a joking way that he knew people so untrustworthy that they could not be trusted to go places, and if they went, they could not be trusted to return.

Snyder told the car to go to a certain service station and get some gasoline and come back.

The car, in the presence of hundreds of people, went down the street without a driver, stopped at an intersection, made a left turn and went out of sight, and was observed to stop at a service station for gasoline.

Several minutes later the car came back up the street without a driver and stopped where Snyder was.

Several hundred people witnessed this unusual spectacle. They all were baffled. None had an explanation for this car that operated upon request of this man called Snyder.

The police came up and told Snyder he was under arrest for disturbing the peace. The people scattered. In the early 1930s, Black people had a fear and a severe distrust of the policeman. During this period in American history, Black people could be arrested for any reason and there was hardly any recourse for justice. So it was understandable that when the policeman came around, no Black person wanted to be around or get involved.

Phillip was skilled in keeping a safe distance from what he considered to be trouble. When the police approached, he retreated to a safe distance from the scene of the arrest. Phillip felt that Snyder was able to take care of himself.

Snyder unshackled himself from the handcuffs and handed them to the police. He told them that the handcuffs were not necessary and that he would go voluntarily. He told the police that he was allowing them to arrest him anyway.

Snyder was locked in a cell in the county jail. The police told the clerk to charge him with disturbing the peace.

The police walked out of the building onto the street, and before he could walk thirty feet away, he heard a voice, "Hey, Sheriff." The police looked back and was surprised and frightened to learn that it was Snyder. Snyder told him that he had forgotten his keys. He handed the cell keys to the police.

The police told Snyder that he would have to put him back in jail. Snyder told him that he would voluntarily go back. Again, the cell door was locked with Snyder on the inside. As the police turned to walk away, Snyder called him, and he looked back to find that Snyder was holding his keys. "You forget them again, Sheriff." The police, with a strange and confused look, accepted the keys, walked away, and called the highway patrol in Montgomery.

The local police told the head of the state patrol what had happened. The head of the state patrol told the local police to "let that damn nigger go before he turned out all the other prisoners." Snyder was released and warned not to cause any more trouble.

Snyder asked how much his fine was. The police told him that if he left town right away, he would not have to pay anything. The police told him to just leave town, and the charges and fine would be dismissed.

Snyder thanked the police and turned around and handed the police the jail keys and said, "You seem to keep misplacing your keys."

Phillip went home that afternoon and told his mother and his younger sister and his brother what had happened. He would never forget the strange unnatural events that took place and the man who did them, Snyder.

The jail could not hold Snyder, and the police could not intimidate him. The people in this small town did not know who he was or where he came from. However, they would never forget Snyder, the Black magician who defied logic, the imagination, and the police.

CHAPTER 4

A Burning Rock You Can't Turn Loose

In the early 1930s, there was a blacksmith shop in the small town of Notasulga. The blacksmith was a heavy-built Black man, with ruddy skin color, called Sweet Peaches. He had scars on his lips and jaws that were said to have resulted from burns he sustained as a small boy while attempting to eat hot candied sweet peaches from a pan from his mother's hot stove.

Sweet Peaches was known for his great physical strength, his skill as a blacksmith, and his affection for children. A blacksmith shapes metals while they are heated to red hot.

The blacksmith shop was a very lively and entertaining place for many people to hang out. People would bring their mules and horses to be shod. Great skill was required in nailing horseshoes on many of these animals, as well as removing the old ones. Many of the mules and horses were wild and unwilling to be shod or unshod. There was also the heating of metals to red-hot temperatures and

Sweet Peaches' rhythmic and musical hammering of these metals to make them pliant.

It was an entertaining act and skill amazing to behold. It was an impressive sight to watch Sweet Peaches carry out his craft as a blacksmith. Sometimes he would say or sing rhymes to coincide with the jingle and banging of his hammer. He knew his craft well. He did it with highly developed skill and artistic precision.

His musical humming and muscular hammering on the red-hot glowing metals combined to fascinate the onlookers. In the winter season, the open fire and the comforting warmth that flowed therefrom was an added attraction.

For these reasons, the blacksmith shop was an attraction for many Black males, young and old. It was a place for youngsters to hang out and listen to what the elders talked about and to see some of the things that they did. Some of the unbroken and untamed horses and mules had to be restrained while they were being shod and unshod with horseshoes.

It was a typical cold day in this small town, and there were about twelve or fifteen men standing around and sitting around at the blacksmith shop. Some were sitting around playing checkers. Others were conversing. Some were watching the blacksmith do his work.

The Black man called Snyder walked into the blacksmith shop, which was mostly an open-shelter-type structure.

Some of the men recognized him and asked him to perform some tricks.

Snyder told them that Sweet Peaches was quite an entertainer himself. Sweet Peaches continued to hammer the metal material.

The men's attention shifted to Snyder. Being the entertainer he was, it was not long before Snyder started doing some unusual things.

He asked a man what time it was. The man pulled out his pocket watch, suspended by a gold chain. Snyder got the watch and reached and got a hammer and started hitting on the watch, smashing it to smithereens.

The owner of the watch got very upset and started talking about the price and value of the watch. Snyder reached down and put the smashed pieces in a handkerchief, waved one hand over the wrapped handkerchief, opened it, and handed it to the owner. The watch was whole, intact, ticking with no loss of time. It was incredible.

There was a man well-known by the group of men at the blacksmith shop. He was called "Buddy." Buddy was known to get intoxicated and use derogatory language. He started using such language in the presence of Snyder. One of the men whispered to Buddy to take it easy because the man he was talking to was Snyder. Buddy stated that he did not give a damn who it was.

Snyder stated to Buddy that it sounded as if he wanted to fight. Snyder stated that he did not want to fight and that he preferred having fun. He tells Buddy to dance until he tells him to stop.

Everyone who knew Buddy was aware that he could not dance. However, at the command of Snyder for him to dance, he obeyed. Buddy started doing some very intricate footwork, resembling tap dancing and country buck dancing.

Although the dancing was funny, the fact that Buddy was actually dancing and did not know how to dance went beyond humor. Buddy continued to dance until Snyder told him to stop.

Snyder asked Buddy if he still wanted to fight. Buddy answered with full sobriety that he had had enough. Buddy seemed somewhat confused, not knowing exactly what had happened to him, especially the rhythmic movement of his feet. He walked away from the blacksmith shop and headed toward home in a state of puzzlement. He could not quite figure out what happened. He was aware of his being under the influence of alcohol when he approached Snyder, but he could not understand how his body, and especially his feet, danced with such rhythm, precision, and balance. Buddy left this scene in a state of confusion. But there were two things he recognized he was no longer intoxicated and his confusion was not due to the alcohol. He had witnessed and participated in something that was unnatural.

Buddy's dancing had caused Sweet Peaches to stop his hammering and join the group. The weather was cold, but a few other persons joined the gathering under this sheltered blacksmith shop.

Snyder used some brown paper and made dollar bills and distributed them to the people standing around. He made money fly. He made quarters and half dollars disappear and reappear. The money could be heard falling in various places, and upon inspection, the money would be where it was heard to fall.

Snyder made candy for the children by just asking them to reach in his hat. As they reached into this hat, they pulled out various kinds of candy.

A sixteen-year-old youth by the name of Denny, who was known to be brash and aggressive, skeptical, and testing, kept making remarks that he did not believe that Snyder could do these things, being witnessed by the group. It was Denny's style to test limits. He would go as far as he would be allowed to go.

Snyder told Denny that he would see if he could be a little more convincing with him. He told

Denny to walk across the street and put his back on the wall.

Denny, without a word and without hesitation, went across the street and turned his back to the wall. Snyder told him to stand there awhile.

Denny's body seemed fixed against the wall. This brash youngster seems transformed into a cooperative and pliant participant with Snyder. Denny could move his hands and eyes, but he could not move his feet.

Denny was being held against the wall by some strange power. He was not in any pain. He just could not move from the wall.

The people watched this brash teenager stand against the wall at the suggestion of Snyder and he could not move from the wall.

Snyder released Denny from the wall by beckoning for him to come to him from across the street.

Denny returned from across the street but in a much more subdued attitude.

Sweet Peaches asked Denny, "Were you really stuck against that wall, boy? Did it hurt you?"

Denny replied, "I could move my hands and eyes, but I couldn't move my feet."

Sweet Peaches was unbelieving. He asked Snyder to do another trick and that he was going to watch Snyder real closely.

The group's attention focused on Snyder and Sweet Peaches as Sweet Peaches prepared to give Snyder a closer look.

Snyder pointed at a rock that was on the ground and told Sweet Peaches to pick up the rock. There was nothing unusual about the rock.

Snyder told Sweet Peaches to examine the rock really well. Sweet Peaches did so. He told Sweet Peaches to pass the rock around to other members of the group.

There was nothing unusual about the rock that was about the size of a golf ball.

Sweet Peaches commented, "I don't see anything different about this rock. Looks like an ordinary rock to me."

Snyder said, "Are you sure?"

Sweet Peaches replied, "Yes, I thought you were going to show a trick."

Snyder then said, "Burn him, rock."

Sweet Peaches yelped, "Hey, this rock is hot. Hey, this thing is hot."

Sweet Peaches started passing the rock from one hand to the other. He was unable to throw it down. He started running around in a trance, blowing his hands as he passed the rock back and forth and exclaiming, "Hey, this thing is hot. Whew, this rock is hot."

The crowd got a big laugh out of watching Sweet Peaches, the blacksmith, run around with a burning rock in his hand that he could not turn loose.

Finally, he told Sweet Peaches to hand him the rock. Sweet Peaches handed the rock to Snyder.

Snyder held the rock in his hand and asked if anyone wanted to touch the rock to see if it was hot.

The crowd backed up. Everyone was afraid to touch the rock.

Snyder tossed the rock aside and left. The crowd was still amazed and amused. Sweet Peaches, now convinced, continued to blow his hands, stating that "That rock was hot, and I couldn't throw it down."

CHAPTER 5

A Circle on the Ground Becomes an Invisible Jail

A group of young Black men were having fun by wrestling with each other at the Notasulga train depot. It was during the fall of the year. There were bales of cotton on the platform to be shipped to various places. It was a popular hang-out for many young men. It was a place to congregate and watch the men haul the bales of cotton and load them on the trains. For many people in this small town of five hundred people, the trains were the most exciting entertainment that they had. It was a natural place to congregate.

Also, it was a place to watch who got on the trains and who got off. Snyder joined the group almost inconspicuously. He stood around and watched several of the wrestling matches. Some of the wrestling matches were very impressive because of the muscular bodies, swift movements, and athletic skills of the participants.

Snyder appeared so ordinary that one of the wrestlers did not know who he was. The wrestler started challenging members of the group to wrestle with him. He was known to be one of the strongest and toughest wrestlers around town. He had a bullying reputation. Most of the men were afraid of him. He was known to threaten and intimidate and even embarrass some of the men in the crowd.

The wrestler asked the group, "Is everybody chicken?" Snyder told the wrestler, "You are strutting like a Rhode Island Red rooster."

This statement got the wrestler's attention. He looked at Snyder and told him, "You must not know who I am."

Snyder laughed and responded by saying, "Friend, just who are you supposed to be?"

The wrestler became angry and said, "That does it."

He proceeded to lunge toward Snyder to attack him, as the other men looked on with interest.

Suddenly and abruptly, the wrestler was stopped, in a frozen position. He was as still as a statue and in a very awkward position leaning forward with his arms outstretched.

After about two minutes, Snyder told the group, "It seems that he is in a very clumsy position. He looks like he is trying to jump on somebody."

The crowd of men standing around laughed at this wrestler standing in the frozen and awkward position. Some looked amazed and puzzled.

Snyder told the man that if he had cooled off sufficiently, he could relax.

The statue-like position of this wrestler who was frozen and immobilized in his tracks regained his composure.

The wrestler stated in a frightened and apologetic voice, "Excuse me, mister, I made a mistake." The man backed away and left.

Each time Snyder appeared there were many persons who wanted to see him do tricks. On this day it was no exception. So, with a background of men carting and loading bales of cotton on trains from the depot platforms, Snyder did a lot of unusual tricks.

He made cotton candy by pulling apart cotton. Many people ate the cotton candy. Cotton candy was very uncommon in this small town. It was usually seen only during carnivals and circuses. However, Snyder made this cotton candy by continuously pulling apart the cotton that was in his hand. Large masses of pink cotton candy were produced in his hand. Many of the people ate the candy. Some were reluctant and withdrew when offered the candy.

The pranks of Snyder (as they were called) attracted a lot of attention. This was great fun, unusual excitement, and high-powered entertainment.

The people's desire for the unusual and for the mysterious had been stimulated. Their expectation to witness the unknown phenomenon had been heightened. They wanted to see more and more of the strange and spectacular powers of Snyder. There was something strange, awesome, and unfathomable about this easygoing Black man. He did these unusual events with ease and ultimate confidence. He was a man who appeared to be in ultimate control of himself and the things he did. He was relaxed. There was a lack of intensity about him. His movements were smooth and sure. He had a casual personality and humor.

Snyder walked down from the depot platform and took a stick and drew a circle on the ground about eight feet in diameter. He told the group that he was going to ask for some volunteers to step inside of the circle and he had a surprise for them.

Snyder asked, "Can I get some volunteers?"

After some reluctance and reservation, four young men walked inside the circle.

One of the young Black men asked Snyder what the surprise was.

Snyder replied, "The surprise is that you cannot get out of the circle until I let you out." They were able to walk around inside the circle, but they could not cross the line to get out of the circle. When they attempted to get out of the circle, it appeared that they were bumping up against an invisible wall.

The four men gave a comical appearance as they walked around inside of the circle trying to get out, but they could not.

Some of the bystanders were enjoying the amusement. Some did not believe that the men could not get out of the simple circle. Some were saying, "I bet I can get out of that circle."

Finally, Snyder told them that they could come out. They walked out with no problem.

Others tried to get out without success.

Finally, three well-known men asked Snyder to let them try it.

John White, Buddy Moore, and Buddy Weems walked inside of the circle. They then attempted to walk back out. They could not get beyond that line no matter how much they tried.

These three men really put on a show because they employed more creativity in trying to get out.

John White tried crawling out. Buddy Moore tried climbing out. Buddy Weems tried to get out by taking a running start only to be stopped abruptly.

The three men attempted to get out unsuccessfully until they got tired and gave up.

Buddy Weems stated, "Man, this place is like a jail. Let me out."

Snyder told them that they could come out. The three men gave a sigh of relief to be out.

Buddy Weems left the scene saying to Snyder, "I am through with you. I am through with you."

The crowd asked for more miracles. Snyder told them that he must catch the next train heading north.

Someone answered and said that the next train did not stop in Notasulga. Snyder told them, "You watch, it will stop for me."

Snyder walked to the waiting place behind the train depot next to the railroad track. The train that was not scheduled to stop was heard blowing about two miles below Notasulga. The group of men and young boys stood watching to see whether the train would stop or keep going as usual. The train continued to blow as it approached the station.

The depot attendant had hung the mail up on a met- al-like post so that as the train passed through the mail it would be snatched from the post without the train stopping. This was interesting to watch also.

In looking down the track, the train had come into view. It was blowing and puffing full steam ahead.

Snyder just stood there near the track anticipating boarding the train.

Suddenly, the breaks on the train started screeching and the train came to a full stop.

The conductors and engineering started inspecting the train to see what was wrong. They checked the wheels and the brake system but could not find anything wrong.

Snyder looked around at the crowd in his usual casual manner. He waved his hand and boarded the train.

And to the amazement of the train conductors and engineers, the train started moving when Snyder got on.

When the people in this small town inquired as to why the train stopped, the word went out that the train stopped for Snyder to get on.

The group of conductors and engineers did not know why the train stopped, but there was a group of people who were convinced that Snyder stopped the train.

CHAPTER 6

A Narrow Escape

The passenger train called "38" pulled into the station at Loachapoka where various persons were waiting to meet certain passengers. Some were there to board the train, and some were just standing around as usual.

The big steam engine stopped its puffing, and the train slowed down as the wheels came to a gradual halt. The conductors, with their black suits and black top hats, stepped down from the train to the ground and went about their duties giving assistance to the passengers who were unloading and those who were preparing to board the train.

The White passengers got off the train from the rear cars, as was the custom. A few Black passengers unloaded from the cars closest to the steaming engine.

A Black man, by the name of Jesro, was among those who were watching the train load and unload. He had a reputation of trying to go with every beautiful Black woman he saw. So naturally, he was watching with interest and anticipation of seeing an attractive woman.

And as fate would determine it, suddenly, one of the most beautiful Black women got off the train. She was well dressed, with long, black, wavy hair and a smooth complexion. Needless to say, this strikingly beautiful Black woman got everyone's attention, although some attempted unsuccessfully not to stare.

Jesro was captivated by this woman. He immediately started searching for some reason or some excuse or some way to acquaint himself with her. Although Jesro had ways that many people disliked, he also had a boldness and aggressiveness that many people admired and envied.

Jesro did not waste much time in approaching this strange lady in town. He went to her and asked her if he could help her with her suitcase while reaching for the suitcase as he made the request.

The woman attempted to be polite and yet resisting Jesro's help, she replied, "No, thank you, someone is waiting for me."

She continued to walk toward the front of the building to the street side where some automobiles were parked. Many people who came to meet the train would park in front of the building on the street and wait for their passengers.

Jesro continued his efforts to get to know this woman as he continued to walk with her without being invited.

"May I please learn what your name is?" Jesro asked.

"Edna Marie."

"Where do you live?"

"Lee County."

The conversation was interrupted by an automobile that drove up to the curb where Jesro and Edna Marie had walked.

Jesro became aware that the man driving the automobile was there to pick up Edna Marie. Therefore, he backed up for fear that she might be a married woman with a jealous husband. And Jesro was well aware of the hazard posed by such a triangle.

The man who got out of the car was Snyder. He got her bags and put them on the back seat of the car and opened the car door for her. She got into the car, as a number of people looked, and recognized Snyder.

General statements were made upon recognition of Snyder and Edna Marie:

"That's Snyder."

"That must be his wife."

"Boy, is she a good-looking woman."

Jesro watched speechless as Snyder and Edna Marie prepared to drive off. His passion for Edna Marie continued to build even after he learned that she was Snyder's wife or friend.

He decided that he must see her again. He felt that this was his opportunity to find out where she lived, and where Snyder lived also. He withdrew from the crowd ran and got into his car and started trailing Snyder and Edna Marie as soon as they drove off.

Jesro kept a safe distance so as not to let them know he was trailing them. After following them for almost seven miles, Snyder drove into a service station along the road.

Snyder asked the White service station attendant to check his air in the tires and fill his tank with gasoline. Jesro parked his car off the road and went near the station and looked out from behind some bushes at Snyder and the activity at the service station.

The White service station attendant was quite unfriendly to Snyder. Snyder was not fit in with the typical role that he felt Black folk are to play. He felt that this Black man seemed beside himself because he was not bowing and scraping and being obsequious. He is wearing a suit of clothing. He is driving a decent automobile and is accompanied by an attractive, long-haired, fair-skinned Black woman. In the mind of this service station attendant, Snyder was trying to act like White folks. These thoughts were irritating to this service station attendant. And his attitude began to show itself.

There were several other White men at the station casting hostile and mockery looks at Snyder.

When the attendant finished pumping the gasoline into Snyder's car, he told Snyder, "Boy, I'm not gonna check your tires. We don't do that for niggers."

Snyder's gasoline bill came to two dollars. Snyder handed the attendant the two dollars, and the attendant snatched the two dollars from the hand of Snyder and told him to leave in a hurry.

Snyder was not leaving fast enough to satisfy the service station attendant, so the attendant beckoned for two of the other White men.

"C'mon, let's teach this nigger a lesson."

Jesro continued to peep from his hiding place in the bushes. He wondered why Snyder would stop at a place like that because this man had a reputation for mistreating Blacks. In fact, this man was known to slap and even kick Black people. Jesro was curious to see what Snyder would do.

Edna Marie was watching with uneasy feelings as the White men increased their intimidations and threats.

Snyder saw that they were determined to gang him. By the time he attempted to get in his car, they started toward him. One of the men had a metal tire tool and the other one had a heavy-duty hammer.

Snyder turned around to face them.

The attendant cursed at Snyder and drew his feet back and kicked at Snyder and missed. His foot swung high in the air and stopped, high in the air. The other two men swung their tools at Snyder, and they became frozen in uncomfortable and awkward positions. The three of them stood like statues in their awkward, clumsy, and uncomfortable positions.

The attendant asked, "What did he do to us? I can't get my foot down."

The other two men stated that they could not get their hands down either, and their arms were tired, but they could not move anything but their eyes and mouths.

Jesro was still looking in disbelief.

Snyder said, "What will it take to stop you from hating people and hurting people because they were born Black?"

"Mister, I have learned my lesson. I will not ever try to kick another colored person again," stated the attendant.

Snyder asked the attendant, "Do you see the position your foot is in?"

"Yes, sir."

"Who put it in that position?"

"I did, but I won't do it again if you let it down,"

Snyder asked the two men holding the tire tools whether they had learned a lesson. They stated emphatically that they had.

Snyder told the attendant, "Put your foot down."

The man, with his right foot high in the air, was released from his frozen position and obeyed Snyder and put his foot back on the ground, where it belonged. Likewise, the other two men lowered their raised hands, with their weapons of war. These men had never been so startled. They had never been so humbled and abased at the hand of a Black man. Their humiliation was increased because they were the cause of it. They exalted themselves, and they were made abased.

The three men walked back to the service station in a state of shock.

Their brains had not completely accepted or processed what had transpired. It happened to them. They experienced it, but it was more like a dream than reality. It would be sometime in the future, if ever, before they could accept the extraordinary happening.

Snyder got into his car and drove off.

In spite of the strange happening, Jesro would not be deterred. He ran and got back into his car and continued to follow Snyder and Edna Marie.

Several miles farther Snyder turned off the main highway onto an unpaved street and drove into a yard with flowers and trees bordered by a fence.

Jesro passed by the house and gave a sigh of relief. Now he knows where the beautiful lady lives, and also where Snyder lives. He also relished the fact that he knew the lady's name-Edna Marie.

Jesro thought to himself, I must see her. I must see her again.

Inside of the house Snyder took Edna Marie in his arms and kissed her, expressing his joy in having her back from a trip that she took to Montgomery. She returned the affection and said, "I missed you too. What did you do to those men at the service station?"

"They were attempting to gang up on me, and I was forced to defend myself."

"When he attempted to kick you, why did you stop his leg up in the air?"

"Often, when people can see how silly they look, they can learn from the experience."

Edna Marie asked, "What do you mean?"

"The man who got his foot stuck in the air, over his head, back there at that filling station can probably explain it much better than I can."

Snyder and Edna Marie laughed.

Edna Marie paused and gave serious thought to what Snyder said as she continued to unpack her bags.

"You know, I had never thought of that. Some folks act crazy because they have never got a good look at themselves while acting crazy."

Edna Marie continued, "But you made those men look at themselves today. They will never forget how they looked either. They looked bad and cheap."

"Yeah, they did. Foot in the air. Hands drawn back, with mean and frowned-up faces. They were really caught in the act, and they were their own eyewitnesses."

Edna Marie started dusting and cleaning the house as they talked. She asked Snyder where the broom was. Things had gotten somewhat disarranged in her absence.

Snyder answered, "Broom, broom, wherever you are, come to the lady of the house."

To the surprise of Edna Marie, the broom came walking across the room to her, upright and unassisted. The broom walked across the room.

"You know, if you were not a good man, I would be afraid when you do things like making brooms walk."

Somewhat compulsive about her housework, she started sweeping the floor and complaining that

Snyder had not done a better job in keeping the house clean in her absence.

"You know how I dislike doing lady's work around the house. By the way, who was that man following you at the train station?"

"I don't know. He wanted to carry my bags, but I wouldn't let him."

Snyder, with a sense of humor, said, "Seems like he wanted to carry more than the bags."

Meanwhile, Jesro had driven around the area where Edna Marie lived to familiarize himself with the streets and the community. There appeared to be no opportunity for him to see Edna Marie on this occasion because Snyder was there. He drove by the house to take one last look before driving back to where he lived. He said to himself, "Jesro, be patient, it's just a matter of time."

Snyder started telling Edna Marie about some of his future planned performances. He expressed excitement about some of his plans to provide spectacular entertainment to children in the schools and other people in the small towns. "I like to see the eyes of children light up and their minds stimulated and excited with curiosity and wonder. I also like to see the common people like us happy."

Snyder continued, "I want to open a door so people can get a look at the possible impossible. It makes them think. It makes them wonder. It makes them happy. It takes their minds away from hard times and depression."

Edna Marie, not understanding fully all the things Snyder was talking about, complained that she was uncomfortable around crowds of people and preferred staying home. She expressed concern about keeping the house clean and looking after her aging parents. She let Snyder know that she did not share his enthusiasm for public entertainment.

"Besides, what do you get out of it?" asked Edna Marie.

"I get enjoyment, satisfaction, a feeling of being alive, and making other folks feel alive, a feeling of giving and sharing. I feel happy when I make other people happy."

"What about those White folks who don't like Black folks going around doing things publicly like you?"

"They don't know enough to hurt me. Besides, many of the White folks enjoy my performances the same as Blacks do."

Edna Marie reminded Snyder about what had happened at the service station. "Things could have been much worse," she said as she reinforced her argument.

Snyder reminded Edna Marie that those three White men learned a lesson that they will never forget.

Edna Marie said, "Yeah, they learned their lesson, but it is still dangerous traveling around in the midst of prejudiced White folks."

Snyder assured Edna Marie that he would be safe and that he would not insist that she travel with him.

He helped Edna Marie with dinner by cooking food without fire and making chipped ice without refrigeration.

After eating the delicious meal, Snyder went into the living room and reclined with his feet elevated on a small table. It is now early evening, and they are preparing to retire for the day. As she entered the room where Snyder was reclining, he requested that she pull off his shoes.

In a playful and good-natured response, she told him, "If you can make a broom walk across the floor, I know you can pull off your shoes, so do it yourself."

Snyder, in a playful mood, told Edna Marie, "You gonna be sorry."

He sat up in the chair and waved his hand and her blouse came off. She laughed and folded her arms to cover herself and said, "Oh, no, you wouldn't dare do that."

She ran toward the kitchen door and the click of the lock could be heard. Edna Marie, still laughing and still attempting to escape, stopped and started running toward another door. The lock on that door also locked with a click. He then waved his hand and her skirt fell down. She reached down and grabbed the falling skirt and continued her determination not to be undressed by his magic.

There was one other door left. She was determined to exit with the remainder of her clothes on. She picked up a glass bowl from a table and threw it up near Snyder, and when he reached out to prevent the falling bowl from breaking, she ran into the bedroom and locked the door from the inside.

He went and knocked on the door, "Let me in."

She answered, "No, you can't be trusted."

He waited until she started dressing for bed and the door clicked unlocked, and she ran and jumped in the bed. And he ran behind her, capturing her with his affectionate embrace. "Now you know you can never escape from me."

They set aside their differences and shut out the world. They created a world of their own that was filled with warmth, tenderness, and joy beyond description resulting from the identity of souls.

Several days later Snyder was performing in a small town in Macon County, and the county sheriff and the local police decided to arrest him.

Snyder told them that he would go to jail, but he would not stay. They put him in a small jail referred to as "the calaboose."

Jesro saw them put Snyder in jail and he said to himself, "This is my opportunity."

He got into his automobile and drove above Loachapoka, where Edna Marie lived. He parked his car on a back street several blocks away from the house. He then walked rapidly toward the house, looking back, right, and left to make sure that no one was watching him.

He finally approached the house with an apprehensive caution. He was fearful. He knew he should not be there. But he was driven by this uncontrollable passion to see Edna Marie. He could not allow negative thoughts or future consequences to enter his mind. He suppressed them because his passion was overriding his rationality.

He knocked on the door not knowing exactly what to expect and not knowing precisely what he should say. As he waited for a response to his knock on the door, thoughts of what he ought to say in such an unpredictable and precarious situation kept running through his mind.

Meanwhile, ten miles away at the Macon County calaboose, the sheriff and local police had put Snyder in this small jail. The jail was made out of brick with small, barred windows at the top. The barred windows were too high to see a person confined from the outside. Sometimes, an outside onlooker could see the hands of the confined persons as they grip the metal bars, in an effort to lift themselves up, to try to look outside.

The calaboose had a large padlock on the outside, and it was completely inaccessible from the inside. Snyder was left in this brick calaboose behind a solid metal door with an outside padlock.

Snyder made some small knocking sounds against the door from the inside and the padlock fell from the door on the outside. He pushed the door open and walked out of the calaboose. He picked up the big heavy-duty lock and walked down the street toward the police station.

The police had just walked into the small office after his return from arresting Snyder. Snyder walked into the police station and the sheriff was completely surprised that Snyder had gotten out of jail. The police first assumed that he had broken out because the police had the only key to the lock.

However, Snyder was holding the opened lock in his hand.

He stated to the police, "I just stopped by to leave this lock with you. There is no damage to the lock. No damage to the door, and no damage to the calaboose."

Snyder handed the lock to the police and walked down the street and got into his car and drove off.

The police went and inspected the door of the calaboose and shook his head in disbelief. He could not accept or believe what he was undeniably witnessing.

Edna Marie opened the door, but when she recognized the face of Jesro, she attempted to close it.

"Please don't close it. I have something to tell you about, about Snyder."

"Okay, make it quick and leave."

"Please, Miss Edna Marie, may I come in?"

She reluctantly opened the door and walked into the living room and asked Jesro to have a seat, but that he must leave soon as possible.

"Okay, mister, you said you had something to tell me about Snyder?"

"Yes, ma'am, I saw him down there in Macon County doing a show on the street."

"Well, so what?"

Jesro was hesitating before getting to the point because he wanted to prolong the time in the presence of Edna Marie. He had not been able to think about anything else since he saw her at the depot. And now he finds himself alone with her. He can barely keep his composure in this awkward situation, because he is not saying or doing what he is thinking or feeling.

"Miss Edna Marie...miss...uh, yes, Snyder's okay...I like you... Can...or, I wonder if I can come see you...?"

"No, you cannot. I belong to Snyder."

She got up and told Jesro, "You better go before Snyder gets back."

"He won't be back for a while."

"Why do you say that?"

"I think the police arrested him."

"He will be back. The jail cannot hold him."

Jesro, being overcome by his passion for Edna Marie, reached out and grabbed her and embraced her and catching her by surprise, attempted to kiss her. He continued to hold her, trying desperately to fulfill his fantasy of kissing her, but she continued to struggle to resist him.

To Jesro's great surprise, Snyder drove up into the driveway.

Jesro heard the car. He turned Edna Marie loose, looked out of the window, and his dreaded suspicion was confirmed: Snyder was out there getting out of the car.

Jesro found himself in a state of panic compounded by a frightening dilemma. He could not wait, and he was afraid to leave. Time had run out. He decided to go out of the back way, crashing through the back door.

Jesro jumped a five-foot fence as he left Edna Marie's backyard. He fell, but with rapid reflex action, he got up and continued to run.

Edna Marie met Snyder at the door, half-frightened, and told him that the man they saw at the depot was there and had run out of the back door.

"Yes, I know. He will be too frightened to bother you again."

"He told me that they arrested you."

"Yes, they did. But you should have seen that police's face when I handed him his jail lock."

Referring to Snyder's arrest and Jesro's uninvited visit, Edna Marie stated that she did not know whether it was better to stay at home or go with Snyder during his performances.

Jesro finally ran in view of his automobile. He had the feeling that Snyder would catch him or have something happen to him any second. However, his car was only a few yards away. But these yards seemed like miles and seconds seemed like hours.

When he finally got into the car, it would not start. He desperately turned the motor over and over, but the engine would not fire. He was convinced in his own mind that it was Snyder who prevented the motor from starting.

He decided on one other last possibility that was made possible because he was parked on an incline. He decided to push the car to get it started.

As he pushed the car, it started gaining speed, almost outrunning him. He barely was able to jump onto the running board of the car and jump through the window to prevent the car from going out of control.

After much wrestling with the steering wheel, he finally gained control of the car. After much frustration and perspiration, the engine finally started. He considered this an answer to a prayer.

Jesro gave a sigh of relief as he wiped his brow with his handkerchief. He promised himself, and he promised Snyder and Edna Marie (in absentia), "I have learned my lesson. For your information, I won't be back."

CHAPTER 7

Do You Know What's in Your Pockets?

A group of people were gathered at a small black schoolhouse about one-third of a mile from the small town of Notasulga. They were watching Snyder perform his unusual acts.

When Phillip entered the wood-frame school building, Snyder was asking the group whether they knew what was in their pockets.

Phillip had seen him before, and he did not want to get too close, so he chose to stay near the rear of the room.

Snyder asked a man in the back of the room, "What do you have in your pockets?"

The man with his denim suit on answered, "Nothing."

"Would you come to the front?" requested Snyder.

The man came to the front and stood near Snyder.

"All of you heard him say that he had nothing in his pockets," Snyder stated.

Snyder reached his hand in the man's coat pocket and pulled out a white potato. He reached in his other pockets and pulled out more white potatoes, to the surprise of the man.

Snyder, still pulling potatoes out of the man's pockets, looked at the people and said facetiously, "This man does not have anything in his pockets."

The crowd laughed.

The man expressed surprise and amazement as Snyder continued to pull potatoes out of his pockets.

Snyder took the potatoes and put them in a bag and told the man, "Be sure to take these potatoes back to that store where you got them."

As the man started to leave, Snyder said, "Wait, I forgot something."

He shook the man's pants leg and saw peanuts come out of his pants leg.

The crowd laughed and so did the man.

"How many of you know what you got in your pockets?" Snyder asked the crowd of people.

Most of the people were reluctant to hold up their hands because they were shy and wanted to avoid being identified. They were not sure what Snyder would have them do. They wanted to remain as inconspicuous as possible and maintain their anonymity.

However, a number of people raised their hands indicating that they knew what they had in their pockets.

He asked one of the hand-raisers, who was a forty-year-old Black man, "What do you have in your pocket?"

The man replied, "I got about seventy-five cents in change in my front pocket and a handkerchief in my back pocket."

Snyder told the man, "Let me hear you shake the money in your front pocket."

The man shook his front pocket and the jingling sound of the money could be heard all over the room.

"You don't have any quiet money?"

The man answered, "No."

"Okay, pull the noisy money out of your pockets, and let us see it."

The man reached his hand in his pocket and pulled out a handful of marbles.

He expressed surprise, embarrassment, and laughter along with the crowd.

Snyder asked him, "Are you still shooting marbles at your age?"

The people in the audience found the discovery of marbles in the man's pocket to be very funny.

"What did you say you had in your back pocket?"

The man answered, "A handkerchief."

Snyder asked him to pull it out of his pocket and show it.

The man began pulling what he thought to be his handkerchief from his pocket, and it turned out to be a pair of socks tied together.

"Whose socks are those?"

"I don't know," said the man.

"Hold up your pants leg," asked Snyder.

The man held up one pants leg and then the other. To his surprise, he did not have on any socks. He was holding his socks in his hand.

Snyder told the man, "Thank you very much. Now, you may put your socks back on."

The man sat down to put his socks back on, but Snyder interrupted him and said, "Not here."

Snyder held his nose with his left hand and pointed out the door with his right hand and said, "Out there."

The man laughed and went outside to put his socks on.

Another man walked down to the front and stated that he had a comb, a wallet, and a pack of cigarettes in his pockets.

Snyder called a second man to the front and asked him, "What did he have in his pockets?"

The man reached in his pocket. Nothing was there. He frantically reached in his other three pockets, and they all were empty.

"Are you sure you did not give them to this man with the long handkerchief?"

"No, he doesn't have them," said the man.

"It won't hurt to check," Snyder asked the man to check his pockets.

The pocketbook, cigarettes, and comb fell from the pockets of the man with the long handkerchief.

The crowd was amused, and they wondered how Snyder had transferred those items to the other man's pockets.

There was a very aggressive woman in the audience who started irritating Snyder by criticizing him in a disbelieving way.

She stated that what he was doing was not real. "You are just using tricks to fool these people," the woman said.

When Snyder could no longer ignore the woman, he told her that he was going to show the people what she was hiding under her coat.

"I am not hiding anything under my coat. You don't scare me," said the agitated woman.

Snyder pulled a big Rhode Island Red hen from under the woman's coat.

The hen started cackling and flapping her wings. Snyder put the chicken down on the floor, and the chicken ran out of the building cackling and flapping her wings.

The woman was so astonished and embarrassed that she quietly retreated into the audience and did not say anything else during the performance.

She expressed a puzzled look. She could not figure out where that hen came from. She saw it happen before her very eyes, but she could not believe it. There was no hen under her coat, she reasoned to herself. And yet Snyder had actually pulled a full-grown hen from her coat.

Snyder asked the audience, "Do you know what's in your pockets or under your coat?"

Snyder made numerous things appear and disappear from people's pockets. He transferred contents from one pocket to another pocket and from one person's pocket to another person's pocket.

He pulled out chickens and rabbits from people's hats, clothing, and pockets. He gave accurate descriptions of the things and the amount of money that people had in their pockets.

Phillip, a youth who witnessed many of Snyder's performances, had a dollar bill in his pocket. He was standing in the back of the room in what he considered a "safe" distance from Snyder. He was amazed at the performance but preferred remaining inconspicuous and uninvolved.

Suddenly, Phillip felt his pocket for his dollar bill. It was no longer there. The dollar bill had disappeared from his pocket.

Somehow Phillip found enough courage to start walking to the front of the room to ask Snyder for his dollar bill. He walked trembling and shaking not knowing exactly what he would say.

Snyder asked, "Young man, what can I do for you?"

Phillip said, "You got my dollar."

"Are you sure?"

"I think so."

"What makes you think I got your dollar? Did you see me get it?"

"That's how I know you got it, because I would have seen anyone else. You do things folks can't see."

"Okay, I'm not going to argue with you, Phillip. Because you were brave enough to come down and ask for your dollar, I am going to give you two dollars."

Snyder handed Phillip two one-dollar bills and suggested that he hold the bills in his hand very tight so that it would not get away from him.

Before Philip returned to his place in the rear, the two one-dollar bills had vanished from his hand.

Snyder gave him assurance that the money was in his pockets.

A man by the name of Glenn was known to be loud and boisterous. He came into the building using profanity.

Snyder kindly told him, "Excuse me, sir. We don't have profanity at these performances."

Glen had a reputation for being bad and intimidating. He was also known to carry a switchblade knife and had cut numbers of people. Glen was under the influence of alcohol and did not know who Snyder was.

Glenn said loudly, "Nobody tells me what to do." And he then reached his hand in his pocket for his knife. He continued to talk boisterously and feeling his pockets for his knife.

The crowd of people suspected that Glenn had lost his knife or that Snyder had gotten it, but they were not sure.

After observing Glenn's frantic search for his knife without success, Snyder told Glenn, "Your knife is not in your pockets. It will be at home when you get there."

"When you sober up, I will let you know where to find it," said Snyder.

In spite, of Snyder's ability to transfer money and goods, there were no reports of any missing or lost items. The people left talking about the amazing things that they had witnessed.

CHAPTER 8

An Unforgettable School Visitor

Snyder and a beautiful woman, described as his wife, visited Crossroads Elementary School in the rural township of Loachapoka. Snyder drove up in the schoolyard, and he and the attractive woman were greeted by the principal of the school, a Black woman in her middle forties.

The principal introduced Snyder to the other two teachers, who were also women approaching middle age.

The principal told the teachers to assemble all of the children in the larger classroom of the three classrooms in the white wood-frame building.

The presence of this man with the dark suit and Stetson hat generated excitement among the students. They marched into the assembly room, taking their seats, so as to get a good view of the unusual visitors.

"Boys and girls," stated the principal, "we have visitors, and I am asking that you display your best behavior. We have a man who will demonstrate to us some very unusual things."

One of the teachers led the students in singing "Lift Every Voice and Sing." The lively and innocent voices of the children rang out the melody and spirit of James Weldon Johnson.

Snyder did not waste any time in getting right into his performance. He walked to the center of the stage and asked one of the teachers, "May I see your watch please?"

She handed the beautiful gold wristwatch to Snyder. He looked at it and then held it up so everyone could see it. And suddenly, he smashed it to the floor. The watch scattered to pieces in every direction.

The teacher who owned the watch exclaimed in surprise and disappointment, "Oh, my new watch. Why did you do that?"

The excitement had begun. The children had their eyes glued on Snyder and the excitement produced by the smashing of the teacher's watch.

Snyder asked several of the students to help him pick up the parts. They picked them up and handed them to Snyder. He put them in a handkerchief and folded the handkerchief from his hands and it disappeared before their very eyes. It disappeared as a water bubble.

The students were not batting an eye. Their imaginations were running wild. They wondered, "Where did the watch go?"

The students and teachers looked amusingly puzzled.

The teacher who owned the watch was curious as well as concerned about her watch.

"Will I be able to get my watch back or another one like it?"

Snyder asked her, "Do you have a pocketbook?"

She answered, "Yes," and opened her desk drawer and pulled her brown pocketbook out of the desk drawer.

Snyder said, "Okay, I am going to walk across the room and turn my back to you."

He walked across the room and turned his back and told the teacher, "Open your pocketbook."

She opened her pocketbook and saw her watch in it, and she expressed amazement, "This can't be. I don't believe it!"

He asked her, "Is that the same watch?"

She answered, "Yes."

He asked her, "Is it running?"

She held it to her ear and answered, "Yes, it is running."

He asked her if it had the correct time.

She looked at one of the other teacher's watches and looked at her own and answered, "It is ticking, and it has the correct time."

The students were bubbling with excitement and wonderment. Their imaginations were stirred. Their curiosity was heightened. It felt good to be at school and witness such unusual happening.

Snyder pulled rabbits and birds out of his hat and told humorous jokes for fun.

He asked each one of the students to take out a clean sheet of paper and tear it into six pieces, and then roll each piece of paper into a ball and put it into a paper bag that was passed around.

The lady with Snyder took the empty paper bag and went down the several rows of students and collected the balls of paper.

Snyder told the lady who was with him to tie a string around the top of the bag and to shake the bag.

After she finished shaking the bag, he told her to untie the bag and put it on the table.

He then told the students to march around the table and get a handful of paper out of the bag.

They marched around, and to their amazement, they reached for paper and got a handful of individually wrapped candy balls.

He also shook his fingers in a trembling manner, and silver bell candy appeared to be coming out of his fingers and falling on the table before him.

Many of the students ate the candy. Some put the candy in their pockets and lunch boxes, to take home to younger brothers and sisters.

Snyder allowed himself to be blindfolded, and he sat with his back to the blackboard.

He asked for volunteers to write words on the blackboard, and he would state correctly the word written, with his back to the board, and with the covering over his eyes.

Snyder asked for volunteers to write a sentence on a piece of paper, fold it, and place it on his head, and he would read the sentence, still with his blindfold on.

Some of the one-sentence statements were humorous, but Snyder's ability to read them was more baffling and staggering to the imagination. The teachers were just as puzzled as the students. He would read correctly the written statements that were written on folded pieces of paper and placed on his head. He did it with a blindfold over his eyes.

Snyder told the students that he would perform one more act before leaving if he could get two volunteers.

He explained to the student that no one would be hurt and that he would not do anything to endanger them in any way. He told them that he was explaining this very carefully because some people get frightened when he performs this act.

Snyder stated that he would exchange two heads for each person without hurting them.

"Can I get two volunteers for this act?"

Finally, one student came forward and then another.

Snyder congratulated the two boys for their courage, bravery, and confidence in him.

He turned to the class and told them, "You see these two boys? I am going to put Joe's head on Fred's body and Fred's head on Joe's body.

The children hollered out and said, "No, no, no."

Snyder considered their wishes and decided not to go through with the head exchange.

It was interesting to note that the two volunteers who came forward were not as afraid as their fellow classmates. The two boys had utmost confidence that Snyder would not harm them. The other students objected to the performance, not so much because they felt their two fellow classmates would be harmed, but because the idea of an exchange of heads was too mind-boggling and too horrifying. The strange complexity of exchanging two heads of fellow classmates was too much of a strain on their rational logic and limited imaginations.

Snyder suggested a more acceptable but still strange idea.

He told the students, "I will select two students and exchange something that belongs to them, but you can't see it. and you can't touch it."

The students exclaimed, "What is that...you can't see it and you can't touch it?"

"Everybody has it. Everybody has a different one. Instead of exchanging heads, I will exchange voices!"

"Exchange voices?" exclaimed the students.

Snyder stated that he would select a girl and a boy, who demonstrated that they could speak clearly and distinctly.

He told them that he wanted each student to demonstrate how well he or she could speak by reciting the following statement: "Greetings to my teachers and fellow classmates, Snyder visited our school."

Snyder went around the room selecting and requesting that each boy and each girl recite the greeting statements.

Some of the students did well in reciting the greeting. Some did poorly. It offered them an opportunity to express themselves, in competition with other students. It was a jovial time for the students. Some of the recitations brought about laughter. Some produced hand clapping. The students had a lot of fun reciting and listening to others recite, "Greetings to my teachers and fellow classmates, Snyder visited our school."

Finally, Snyder selected a girl and a boy student who appeared to have recited the greeting most distinctly.

The students clapped their hands, applauding the choices of the two students, Eloise and Robert. The classroom was alive with the gaiety of smiling faces, white teeth, bright eyes, and excitement. These students had never been so amused, entertained, or dazzled by such unusual excitement.

These students were from poor Black families, and their deprivations were many. However, on this day, the most important place was Crossroad School, and the most important event was the extraordinary performance of Snyder.

Snyder asked Eloise to stand on one side of the room, and he asked Robert to stand on the other side.

Snyder walked to the rear of the room so that the students could focus their attention on Eloise and Robert, the two students chosen, as the top reciters of the greeting.

"I will ask each of you to repeat the greeting statement that you made to your teachers and fellow students earlier, and then we will ask each of you some questions."

He asked Robert to start first.

Robert began the recitation, and a strange and bewildering thing happened.

The students saw the movement of Robert's lips, but the voice coming from those lips was the voice of Eloise.

They were startled. They were looking and listening, but what they observed was so out of the ordinary that they could not believe their eyes or their ears.

Eloise's voice was not coming from her because her lips were not moving, and she was on the opposite side of the room.

Eloise expressed surprise also to hear her voice coming from the lips of her classmate, Robert.

"Thank you, Robert, for your recitation," said Snyder, who was standing in the back of the room.

"Eloise, please recite the greeting statement to your fellow classmates," Snyder requested.

Again, the same strange thing happened. As she spoke, the voice of Robert came from her moving lips. And yet Robert, on the opposite corner of the room, was not saying anything.

The amazement and suspense among the students mounted. They could not figure out how the voices of Eloise and Robert were being interchanged. Neither of them was a ventriloquist. And the exchanged voices were clear and unmistakable.

The thing that was most puzzling to the teachers and students was the fact that it was only the voice of each student and not the speech or thoughts of the other as was revealed when Snyder questioned each one of them.

He asked them questions that only each of the two students could answer for him and herself. Such questions were birthdates, hobbies, favorite foods, likes and dislikes, and future plans.

Eloise and Robert would answer the personal lines of questions spontaneously, in the voice of the other.

This was strange and confusing to the students, but also fascinating.

Snyder chose two students with distinct-sounding voices. Eloise had a high-pitched voice, and Robert had a low and heavier voice.

Snyder reverted the two students' voices to their natural sounds.

He congratulated the students on their good behavior and thanked them for their participation.

Snyder thanked the principal and the teachers. He bade the students farewell.

The principal asked the students to show their appreciation for Snyder. All of the students stood and clapped their hands and chanted, "Greetings to my teachers and fellow classmates, Snyder visited our school and made us happy today."

CHAPTER 9

Survived the Crushing Wheels of an Automobile

It was truly a nature-filled spring day at the farmhouse of Mr. Will Blake. The sun was beaming its utmost brilliance. The enrichment and splendor of nature were everywhere. The pleasant breeze played with the leaves on the big oak trees. Plants were budding, and flowers were in their picturesque array of blooms.

The Blake house was reminiscent of the Garden of Eden with its trees and orchards of fruits, grapes, plums, peaches, pears, figs, pecans, walnuts, hickory nuts, and various other kinds of fruits, nuts, and vegetation. It was a big unpainted wood-frame house supported with tall brick pillows high enough from the ground to allow the goats, dogs, turkeys, and sheep to go underneath.

The Blake house had a front porch that extended from one side of the house to the other. There were many chairs, and two swings suspended from the porch ceiling. There were straight chairs, rocking chairs, and benches. Most of the chairs, swings, and benches were occupied. Children and adults also sat on the wide eight layers of steps adjoining the porch. Red, white, and pink roses surrounded the porch.

Other people were also scattered and grouped in various activities throughout this spacious, clean, swept yard with outdoor chairs, benches, and swings suspended from the trees with ropes and chains. Colorful flower beds were spread throughout the yard.

The singing birds, the playing children, and the exchange of pleasantries among verbose and laughing adults gave an atmosphere of gaiety to the people milling around this house, which was located within the extraordinary splendor of nature.

During the 1930s Blacks had very few public places to meet. They had a few schools and churches. However, the home was the primary meeting place, when Black people had the time, for leisure and recreation.

It was an exciting experience to visit the Blake house. Mr. Blake and his wife had six strong sons and three beautiful daughters. They were known for their talent, hard work, and industry.

The Blakes had chicken, geese, ducks, turkeys, horses, mules, cows, pigs, goats, rabbits, and squirrels. Many of these animals roam freely around the yard. Some were fenced in.

This home was a natural gathering place for people to come sit, talk, and play, even if they were not entertained, by the Blake family. Invitations were not necessary.

On this sunny Sunday afternoon, the air was clean and filled with the aroma of flowers, tulips, honeysuckles, and magnolias. The Black people were at peace with each other. This peace blended with nature's beautiful harmony. It was a great time to be alive. Music and magic were in the air.

Phillip was playing horseshoes along with several other young teenage boys, when they observed a large, shiny Buick automobile turned off the unpaved road, onto the long unpaved driveway, that led into the big yard at the Blake home.

The driveway to the Blake home had a wooden fence on either side. Horses and other farm animals were behind the fenced-in areas.

The approaching automobile traveled fifty yards from the road to the big front yard, where people were sitting around, standing around, and where children were playing a variety of games.

Phillip and other young teenage boys were playing horseshoes. But when they saw the car approaching, they threw the horseshoes down and mounted their tom walkers, which elevated their height at least two feet and began walking toward the automobile which had come to a stop. The homemade stilts were very popular among many of the youth.

Snyder emerged from the automobile and greeted the young children who came around his car.

Some of the people recognized who he was, and they started asking him to do some tricks.

Phillip could not remember when he had so much fun. He had played with the animals. He had been in the high tree swingers, on the homemade merry-go-round, the seesaw, the bouncing boards, and the tom walkers. He had watched the other children play, including the pretty girls who were dressed in their best Sunday outfits.

And in addition to all of this, Snyder has come by, in his big dark-colored automobile, which became the center of attraction.

Black-owned automobiles were rare in this small rural township in the 1930s. An automobile was a novelty within itself. For many young people, it was the highlight of their whole day to ride in an automobile.

Snyder's automobile was a marvel and a fascination, but Phillip and the other young people were not eager to get too close to Snyder or his automobile.

Snyder invited anyone who wished to do so to get a close-up inside and outside look at his car.

"Anyone wants to inspect this car, you are welcome to do so," Snyder told the people at the Blake home.

One man decided that he would get a closer look. He walked in front of the car and attempted to open the hood, and the front lights started blinking. The man backed up, and the lights went out and stopped blinking.

Apparently, the man thought maybe it was his imagination, and therefore, he approached the front of the car again and reached for the hood.

Suddenly, the front lights along with the fog lights started blinking in rapid succession as the man reached for the hood. Abruptly, he withdrew and stepped back several feet, surprised and puzzled.

The people laughed at this man's skepticism, apprehension, and fright.

Another man walked to the back of the car, and as he got near the bumper, the engine of the car started. And for fear, the car might back into him, he jumped back.

Snyder was standing near the car along with the other people expressing amusement.

The windows of the car were rolled down. One of the men looked through the window of the car. In order to get a better look, he stuck his head in the window and the horn started blowing.

The man jerked his head back and said, "I have had enough of this car."

Snyder assured the people that the car would not harm them. He further advised them that the car was just having fun.

Snyder told the people how obedient his car was, and he proceeded to demonstrate to them. The car would do whatever Snyder commanded.

He was standing on the outside of the car with no one in it. He told the engine to start and it started. It also cut off at this command.

"Move forward." The car moved forward.

"Stop and move backward." The car stopped and moved backward.

The doors of the car opened and closed as Snyder commanded.

"Horn, blow three times." The horn on the car blew three times, with a rhythmic chant to the horn.

"Blow one time." Horn obeyed.

"Two times." Horn obeyed.

"One plus two times." Horn obeyed.

"One time a long time." Horn obeyed.

"One time long, two times short." Horn obeyed.

The people were in speechless awe as they witnessed the spectacular rhythmic timing of the blowing horn responding to the voice of Snyder.

Some of the women and smaller children stood on the big porch and watched Snyder make his car operate by a strange remote control unheard of and impossible to conceive.

A man by the name of Avery drove into the Blake yard. His car was about the same size as Snyder's car. Avery joined the group of people that surrounded Snyder.

Snyder was asking for a volunteer to let his car run across his chest. He assured them that they would not be hurt.

Finally, a man walked up to Snyder and said, "I'll do it. Let it run over my chest."

It was well understood that the weight of Snyder's car would crush a man's ribs.

The man was instructed to lie on the ground in front of Snyder's car.

"Are you ready?" asked Snyder.

"Yes, I'm ready," answered the man.

Snyder told the car to run over the man's body. The car proceeded toward the man. The man became frightened and jumped up.

A second and more determined volunteer came forward.

"Are you sure that it won't hurt me?" said the second volunteer.

"You have my word," affirmed Snyder.

The man lay in front of the car. He closed his eyes and clenched his fist.

The people were intensely concerned and apprehensive.

The front and rear wheels on one side of the car ran across the man's body in rapid succession.

The man jumped up unhurt.

A sigh of relief was expressed by the crowd.

The man could not believe that the car had run over him. He was not injured and said he did not feel the weight of the car. The man or the people observing could not understand why the car did not crush him to death.

Snyder stated that he would volunteer to let Avery drive his car across his body.

Avery stated that his car would crush any man's body to death.

Snyder again assured Avery that the car would not harm him.

Avery expressed reluctance to drive his car over the body of Snyder because he did not want to be responsible for killing anyone.

Snyder told Avery that he was making this request that he drive the car over his body in the presence of all the people who would be witnesses for him if anything went wrong.

Avery agreed to drive his car over the body of Snyder.

Snyder pulled off his coat, shirt, and undershirt so everyone could see that he had no protective covering.

He lay down in the pathway of Avery's big automobile and asked him, "Are you ready?"

Avery was still nervous and reluctant but decided he would go through with it.

Avery replied, "I'm, I'm ready when you are."

He cranked the car and started driving toward Snyder's chest and stomach area.

Some of the onlookers turned their heads as Avery approached Snyder's outstretched body. Others wanted to turn away, but the spectacle of what was taking place was too overwhelming.

The two tires on the right side of the automobile ran across Snyder's body. The bumping and bouncing of the car could be seen and heard as it ran across Snyder's body.

Snyder lay still for a few seconds and then jumped up.

The crowd applauded him for his escape from the crushing wheels of the automobile.

He held up his hands and turned around to show the group that he was not injured.

The people saw it, but they could not believe their eyes.

After Snyder had left and the neighbors started leaving for their different homes, Phillip walked down the road to his house, thinking to himself how beautiful life was. He felt that it was so good to be alive! His imagination had been stimulated! His emotions were bursting with excitement and good feelings!

To him, the plants, flowers, animals, the people, the games, activities, and the man Snyder, and even the air, the sky, and now the beautiful sunset combined to give him a perfect day.

In his mind, he somehow related this to something he had heard a preacher say, "The heavens declare the glory of God, and the firmament showeth his handiwork."

CHAPTER 10

Snyder Escapes from the Mob

One of the White merchants walked into the Auburn Police Department and told the chief of police, "That Negro who plays them tricks is over there on Broad Street. A gang of other Negroes and some White folks are looking at 'em. This kind of thing doesn't look good."

In the early 1930s, it was against customs and traditions for a Black man to affirm himself as a man with the capability of standing up in this Southern town and entertaining Black and White folks. This was disturbing to the White merchant. He came to the police department to invoke the powers of the police to put a stop to this street entertainment by a Black man.

The White chief of police gave immediate assurance to the merchant that something would be done. "We better get somebody over there to see what's going on. Meanwhile, I will git some of the boys together in case we need some help."

The chief of police went outside the office onto the street and called four or five White men who were standing around. He asked them to come into the office.

The chief gave a briefing to several police officers and the men who walked in from the street: "The Negro who plays them tricks is over on Broad Street doing some pranks. A bunch of Negroes and some White folks are watching him and doing a lot of loud laughing. It doesn't look good. We gonna have to do something about it."

One of the men responded, "Yeah, if one Negro starts entertaining White folks and Blacks, it might give other Negroes ideas, and before you know it, things will get out of hand."

Another White man told the group, "Something needs to be done. Just the other day a Negro by the name of Joe Louis knocked our Maxy Baer, a White, somewhere up north. Lots of Negroes talking about it. Some acting uppity. Things like that will make Negroes feel like they are good as White folks. We can't have that kinda thing in the South."

The police chief gave instructions to several of the men to go over there and watch Snyder. He told the others to call their friends and meet back there within the next hour.

Several of the White men walked several blocks to where Snyder was performing. They found about forty or fifty Black and White people gathered around watching Snyder do incredible things and enjoying it.

Snyder held up a fifty-cent coin in his hand, showing it to the people. He then started throwing the coin up in the air several feet high. Each time he threw the coin up an additional coin would be added mysteriously. As he continued to throw the coins up, they increased to the point where he had both hands juggling a string of coins. The coins gave the appearance of a silver spring expanding and contracting, up and down with elastic rhythm and the sound of jingling money.

When he stopped bouncing the coins, they vanished as they fell into the palm of his hands. He had the one coin left that he started with. He held it up to show to the crowd then blew it, and it vanished also.

The people exclaimed and expressed their amazement and wondered where those coins came from and where they went.

Snyder made candy for the children by shaking his hand. The silver-bell-wrapped candy appeared to be coming from his fingers, as he dangled them over a hat where the candy was falling. He distributed it to all the children, who reached out for it. Both Black and White children were amused and reached out for the candy.

A White man who was among the group expressed appreciation to Snyder, in the presence of all the people gathered. "This colored man has provided us and our children a lot of fun with his unusual tricks. Let us pass our hats and take up a collection for him."

Two of the men sent by the chief of police looked at each other in a disgusting and disapproving manner as the money-collecting hats passed through their hands.

Snyder expressed his thanks for the collection but declined to accept the money and suggested that it be given to a poorly equipped local Black school.

Several other men whom the chief police had deputized joined the group. Some members of the group began to sense that the police were getting involved. Uneasy feelings started developing.

This money feeling caused some of the Black people to begin to withdraw from the gathering. Their keen instincts and sensitivity to the changing social atmosphere of the group served as a signal that something unpleasant and dangerous was about to happen. The carefree spirit and laughter of the group had diminished.

A White man came up to Snyder and told him that he would have to leave. Snyder told the man that he was not breaking the law, was not doing anything wrong, just having fun, and that he was not quite ready to leave yet.

This confrontation caused others to start withdrawing quietly from the group. These were peace-loving people, and they would go out of their way to avoid trouble.

The White man knew that he had a number of like companions in the group, and this served to encourage him to become demanding and insulting toward Snyder. The insults turned to threats.

The White man who was verbalizing the threats was joined by another White man. The two men started advancing toward Snyder. One of the men slapped at Snyder, and the other man simultaneously kicked at Snyder. They both missed.

The man whose hand slapped at Snyder and missed swung around and started slapping his own self. Likewise, the man whose foot kicked and missed started swinging back and forth, bending, and kicking his own self. The people looking on were shocked and confused and could not understand why the two men were slapping and kicking themselves.

The people were looking on in amazement at a man slapping his own face and another one kicking himself behind. This had become entertainment within itself. For a few moments, the people were caught up in this slap- ping-kicking spectacle.

After a minute or so, Snyder told the two men to stop. The hand stopped slapping, and the foot stopped kicking.

Snyder told the two men, "You have slapped and kicked yourself. I am going to ask you to do something much more pleasant. I want both of you to dance until I tell you to stop."

The two men started dancing, moving their feet, jumping up and down, swinging their arms, and turning their heads from side to side with vigorous rhythmic motion.

After a minute or so, Snyder told the two men that they could stop dancing if they had learned their lesson.

Some of the people started laughing. Some were too shocked and startled to laugh.

The two men stopped their dancing and were almost breathless after their vigorous display of country buck dancing, typical of the dancing done by many talented Black dancers.

Snyder said, "There is a rule that says that we should not do unto others what we do not want done unto us. If we do not want to be slapped or kicked, let us not slap or kick others. I hope these two men will be better human beings after the valuable lesson they have learned this evening."

By that time the chief of police came to the scene with a number of other White men carrying guns. The chief pulled out his gun and pointed it at Snyder.

The remainder of the people standing around retreated to a safe distance from the scene of this frightening confrontation.

Snyder did not display any excitement. However, the policeman was shaking with fright. His hand and his voice were trembling as he tried to communicate to Snyder that he was under arrest.

"You might want to take a look at your gun before you decide to pull the trigger, Mr. Police," stated Snyder.

The chief of police looked at his gun, and he watched the barrel of the gun curve in his direction until it aimed at him. The chief of police became frightened and threw the gun to the ground. At this time, other police reached for his holstered gun, but the gun jumped out of the holster into the hand of Snyder.

On the scene with Snyder now stood the chief of police, several other police officers, and about twenty-five or thirty angry, frightened, and confused White men. The other people had moved blocks away. They were dazed and stunned. They were attempting to comprehend and cope with the incredible bending of the chief's gun; the gun that jumped out of the other policemen's holster; and the slapping, kicking, and dancing incidents.

While these men were in this confused state, Snyder walked across the street. His car was several blocks away. It was getting along toward sundown. The fun was over. He wanted to get out of town.

The dazed group of men, angered, frustrated, and humiliated, started mobilizing for mob behavior and irrational actions against Snyder. One of the men hollered out, "He is trying to get away. Shoot him!"

One of the policemen shot at Snyder. The bullet bounced back and hit a street sign next to the policeman who fired the shot. The policeman was not sure where the bullet came from, so he fired again. The bullet came zooming back in the direction of the policeman, again hitting the sign next to him. He was then convinced that his own bullets were coming back to get him.

Several of the other policemen shot at Snyder, and their bullets started bouncing back in their direction. The men started ducking and dodging the ricocheting and bouncing bullets. They stopped shooting their guns and took out their clubs.

The mob started moving toward Snyder. "Get after him. Don't let him get away."

Snyder started walking rapidly in the direction of his car. The mob of men started closing in on him, with sticks, blackjacks, and clubs. They were yelling angry and threatening remarks.

Several of the men reached Snyder as he was turning a street corner. They started hitting him frantically and fiercely, as he went down on his knees. The others joined in the beating.

Finally, as they beat him with their sticks and clubs, he fell to the ground as the converging mob unleashed their blind aggression and uncivilized brutality.

As Snyder fell to the pavement, a strange thing happened. His hat fell off and his body tumbled over. There was no head under the hat.

The White men became horrified. Not only was there no head under the hat, but the men learned that they were beating on clothes that were stuffed with dirt. The clothes turned over, and dirt started pouring out of the collar of the coat and shirt.

The men started backing up, looking on with fear and disbelief. The shoes were filled with dirt. Dirt was crumbling from both pants legs. These men, with their sticks and clubs, recoiled in horror.

As they stood speechless, they heard his voice coming from the dirt-filled clothes. "Are you satisfied with beating on my Black body of earth and dust? Are you disappointed because your thirst for blood was not satisfied? What do you seek to destroy, and why do you seek to destroy it? Is it this visible dark dust that you hate or the invisible soul that it houses?"

Their stunned minds and state of shock were interrupted by the opening of the car door on Snyder's automobile. They watched the door open. They saw no one open it. They watched and heard the door close shut. They saw no one close it.

The voice spoke again, this time from the automobile. "Oh, White men, when will you learn that Black men are also made in the image of God? They have minds, souls, spirits, and feelings. Do minds, souls, and spirits have colors? Do you know the color of the wind? What color is daylight?"

The car drove off without a visible driver.

The men looked at each other with a mixture of disgust, shame, fear, and confusion. They dropped their heads and walked slowly in the direction of the police department.

EPILOGUE

Positive magical entertainment excites and intrigues the imagination. It sometimes brings needed stimulation to stagnated minds and imaginations. Wonderment triggers the mind to search for unknown answers and unknown components, to find answers, to solve problems, to find solutions, and to stimulate the creative imagination. To see things in a positive sense that seem impossible and incredible can be very amusing. These were some of the effects that the magic of Snyder had on his audience.

We must be reminded that we live in a mysterious world that surrounds us constantly with mystery and magic. How does a clear, sunny blue sky transform into wet rain, solid hail, ferocious winds, white snow, dark clouds, roaring thunder, and flashes of lightning?

God has created an unceasing dynamic universe replete with wonders, marvels, and mystery. This wonderful, generous, loving God shares his wonders with mankind.

A psalm of David alludes to this in Psalm 8:3-4 (KJV), "When I consider thy heavens, the work of thy fingers, the moon and the stars, which thou has ordained; What is man, that thou art mindful of him? and the son of man, that thou visitist him?" The psalmist in 139:14 says further, "I will praise thee; for I am fearfully and wonderfully made: marvelous are thy works; and that my soul knoweth right well" (KJV). The books of Genesis, Exodus, and Daniel make references to magicians along with wise men and astrologers. It was the magicians who told Pharaoh that the plague of frogs and lice in Egypt was "the fingers of God" (Exodus). It is interesting that the magicians were the ones to call the attention of Pharaoh to the existence and participation of God in this unusual plague of frogs and lice in Egypt. These magicians of Egypt acknowledged God and the power of God beyond the power of the magicians.

The implication of God believing magicians in Egypt gives moral and ethical credibility to the Alabama Black magician known as Snyder. Also, the Pharaoh's acknowledgment of the knowledge and wisdom of the magicians provides credibility for the intelligence and advisory capacity of the magicians of Egypt.

Nebuchadnezzar, king of Babylon, referred to Daniel as Belteshazzar, master of the magicians (Dan. 4:9). The Bible portrays the role and social status of the magician as a person with extraordinary powers and as an advisory consultant to pharaohs and kings. In early biblical history, the pharaohs and kings called upon wise men, magicians, and astrologers to interpret and solve difficult problems.

In the modern era, the limited information available regarding magicians is limited primarily to their ability to entertain with unusual spectacular feats. The spectacular magical happenings by the magician seem to overshadow other information regarding the personal life and person of the magician. People usually focus on what the magicians do and not who they are as persons.

It would probably be an informative adventure to go behind the scenes of the magical activities of the magician, to learn the hidden secrets of his sleight of hands, hypnotic, and illusionary effects. Such adventure behind the scenes of the magical productions of the magicians sounds interesting. However, this undisclosed and unexplained mystery of magic is what makes it entertaining and fascinating. It is reasonable to conclude that the shrouded secrets of magic are a natural part of its nature and significance.

The significance of this Black American heroic magician is illustrated by its indelible impact on the mind of a child (and many other persons) who would take the time to investigate and write about it after seventy-five years. The impressions that I learned about this Black American magician were fascinating, entertaining, inspiring, and positive. I am not going to allow the negatives that I don't know to prevent me from sharing the positives that I do know. Since I do not know any negatives about Snyder, I am not inclined to search for nor invent any negatives on my own. The legends of Snyder are real.

The magicians and magicians are not foreign to biblical knowledge. There are sixteen references to the words magician and magicians in the Bible. They are found in the Old Testament: in the books of Genesis, in the books of Exodus, and in the books of Daniel. This indicates that the history of magicians goes back to the ancient world and that they have played significant roles in human history.

The biblical roles of magicians in the Bible help to create a more meaningful social context for Snyder and the roles that he played, in his entertainment and magic in Alabama. It may be helpful to explore and learn more about the roles and persons behind the magic of the magicians. God has a purpose for all of his creation. There may be some value in studying the roles, purpose, and meaning of the magician.

The legends of Snyder have the potential to create new interests, curiosities, and motivations for research and study of magic and magicians as meaningful, relevant social phenomena. It is an enticement and challenge for the public theologians, psychologists, sociologists, and social scientists to take a closer look at the magicians and their magic, especially in the twenty-first-century technological marvels and mysteries.

Jesus was not known as a magician; however, he was a miracle worker. The miracles that Jesus performed exceeded the feats of all magicians in history. Jesus multiplied five fish and two loaves of bread and fed five thousand people. He changed water to wine. He caused a fig tree to wither with exceeding rapidity. He healed the sick. He gave sight to the blind. He walked on the water. He ordered the raging storm to be peaceful and still. He healed lepers, and he raised Lazarus from the dead. Nicodemus, a ruler of the Jews, came to Jesus by night to acknowledge that no man could perform the miracles that Jesus did, except it is from God,

Where did Snyder get this strange power to perform magical happenings? They were not ordinary happenings. or events. They were extraordinary. I know of no one who could look behind the scenes to see or explain these extraordinary happenings in rural Alabama by a Black American man known as Snyder.

When placed in the context of the deep south of the state of Alabama in the 1930s and 1940s, the legend of Snyder is an extraordinary story. The state of Alabama and the Southern United States were rigidly, racially segregated. However, Snyder was able to perform in the small township streets before racially mixed audiences. He was able to salvage some resemblance of personal dignity and respect as an entertainer, even as a Black American man.

Snyder demonstrated the power of influence of entertainment to get the public's attention and provide a positive diversionary amusement. Positive amusement has the potential to stimulate the mind and provide recreation from the toil of labor and the customary mundane routines of daily living. It is a way to add enjoyment to life without the intake of alcohol, other harmful drugs, and abusive and harmful activities. The legends of Snyder illustrate the potential for mental, emotional, social, and other wholesome benefits from the entertainment of a Black magician even in a segregated oppressive society.

Willie James Webb
Theological Ethicist

ABOUT THE AUTHOR

I am the middle child of seven children born to loving parents in Macon County, Alabama in the township of Notasulga, AL, with Tuskegee being the county seat where Booker T. Washington founded Tuskegee University in 1881. I attended two Rosenwald elementary and junior high schools that were built for Black American children in the segregated South. Both schools were located on the premises of Black Baptist churches, in Shiloh, and Macedonia. I graduated from the eighth grade as valedictorian. I was bussed ten miles to Tuskegee Institute High School and graduated as the president of my senior class.

Macon County was primarily rural, and racially segregated with agriculture as the primary industry. However, it was educationally and culturally enriched due to the massive contributions of Booker T. Washington and George Washington Carver. This enriched educational, industrial, social, and religious culture permeated Macon County, Alabama, America, and beyond. As an early truth seeker, I joined Macedonia Baptist Church as an elementary school child. In my second year at Morehouse

College, I was licensed and ordained a minister of the gospel at Macedonia. I benefited from this rich Black culture that stressed church worship, biblical study, love of God, family, neighbor, and country. These were motivating and inspiring incentives that engendered faith, hope, and success for the future.

My wife Wilma and I were married in 1960. We have one beautiful angelic daughter, Karen. God blessed me to be the interim pastor of Wheat Street Baptist Church and founder and pastor of Foundation Baptist Church in Atlanta, Georgia. I received the Georgia Governor's Award, CEO of the Christian Institute of Public Theology, and the Christian Association of Public Theologians. I am blessed to be the author of six books. I consider myself a public theologian, ministering the whole gospel for the whole person, for the whole world.

Willie James Webb